THE YEAR OF COOKING FISH

Bruce Colbert

The Year of Cooking Fish
© 2025 Bruce Colbert
Cover Art- Kevin Jordan

ISBN- 978-1-961043-15-2

Published by:

Blue Jade Press, LLC

Blue Jade Press, LLC
Vineland, NJ 08360
www.bluejadepress.com

CHICAGO

The Chicago skyline driving north along Lake Shore Drive was constantly changing, newer high-rise buildings pushing up well past 50 stories. One or two were built by my wife Alice's architectural firm that went from being a leader in the design business to an empty shell, doing mostly small-scale projects these days. Within the last five or six years, they had gone through waves of layoffs. The present owner seemed to be counting the days when he could turn the remnants of the firm's greatness over to his son, who had only left architecture school the year before.

I picked my wife up in front of the firm's stylish Victorian building on Erie Street. We were heading home to our townhouse in the DePaul University neighborhood. The conversation in the car was mostly about her discomfort at work. Surprisingly she announced in a voice not really her own, gently slapping my arm, "I'm quitting. Next week." A broad smile quickly dashed across her face. "I'm serious this time," she added. With that, the subject ended as we drove onto Bissell Street before it hits Webster, luckily finding a parking spot ten steps from our front door.

She loved architecture from the beginning. She took drafting courses for extra credit in her suburban high school. Then she declared her interest in the profession on the very first day at the university. When I met her, she was working at the once large firm as an associate. She made working drawings of buildings done by other more prominent architects.

"It was expected of all newbies," she told me over drinks at Butch Maguire's.

Butch Maguire's was an Irish bar on Division Street, where legions of professionals stopped for a drink after work. They usually gathered in clusters of coworkers for protection or for the appearance. That way someone didn't appear to be looking to hook up for the night, which if people had been honest, they were. Everybody then was in their late twenties or early thirties. She was twenty-seven, and I was thirty-four. We were married three years later on her thirtieth birthday. She had chosen the date so I would remember it. Her logic was that you could not forget a woman's birthday and wedding anniversary if they are on the same day.

She always said that it was my wry sense of humor that won her over. She had pushed in next to me at the bar to buy a round for her and the two girlfriends that were sitting behind us at a table. I told her a sort of inane joke based on a silly play of words about Roy Rodgers. I remember she raised her head of long dark hair laughing loudly, so much so that she began to hiccup uncontrollably. Then she belched once to stop it, took out a pen from her business jacket, and wrote her name and telephone number.

"Call me. I want to hear more. You promise?" she said and told me she needed to go with her friends to dinner after this last drink. As she stood facing me with the three drinks on a small tray, she smiled widely and said, "I like a man who's funny." Walking away, she waved and joined her seated friends.

With a grin on my face, I picked up the damp napkin she had written on from the wet wooden bar and stuffed it into my jacket. I drank the last of my beer and headed out the door. Looking back at her, I saw she was telling her friends a story at the table. Her face was animated, possibly about our meeting at the bar, all without noticing that I was leaving.

I didn't call her for two days. I should mention that a good many young women in those days would find me unsuitable. They were looking for a mate with the same small life experience outside of college who might also be marriageable. I could be considered tarnished for someone like this winsome Chicago architect because I had already been married. I was divorced with a daughter who lived with her mother in Memphis.

The telephone number she gave me was her office line and the front desk connected me to her. We bantered a bit on the phone for perhaps two minutes and she said she had to go. We agreed to meet for a drink at a less crowded bar on the Northside. It was connected to a French restaurant named Frere Jacques across from Lincoln Park on busy Clark Street. It was roughly four blocks from where we both lived. She lived in a renovated brownstone with exposed brick walls and a new gourmet kitchen. I lived in a studio about the size of a broom closet. The reason for that hovel was obvious; half my hard-won money went to Memphis.

I had an English friend who enjoyed Frere Jacques and we would often eat at the bar. Philippe the owner had a well-stocked cellar and his wines were usually good. I suggested we meet there, and she cheerfully agreed. "I walk past it all the time, but I've never gone inside. It'll be fun."

Later that evening I arrived at the restaurant before her, a habit in promptness left over from military service. The owner, Phillippe, who also worked the bar, greeted me. I told him I was meeting a lady for drinks for the first time and asked him to wish me luck. "Bien sur," he said. I sat at the far end of the mahogany bar where it curves, a bit more private.

Not long afterward, I saw the door open and a tall dark-haired woman walked inside. She was wearing a powder blue sweater dress with a burnt orange silk scarf. She glanced around for a moment, and noticed me at the bar. She hurried over. We shook hands and she moved to the barstool next to me. Beaming, Philippe was there in an instant and put on his best Gallic charm, praising me as a remarkable man. I shook my head with disbelief, smiling all the while at this absurdity.

Alice chose a strong Cabernet and as she took her first swallow, she turned to me, and exclaimed, "I can taste France." Then laughed, adding, "That sounds a bit silly, doesn't it?"

We talked about the usual first date subjects: family, school, work and Chicago itself. It made for an easy conversation. I felt no need to impress her though I wondered in what way I might. She was smart, reasonably successful, and aware that she was attractive.

As a second round arrived, we decided to eat something and ordered a plate of snails. She ate carefully and sparingly, eating two out of the eight on the plate.

"First or second time with these?" I matter-of-factly asked, guessing that it was her first.

"You found me out," she said, "It was all I could do to swallow them. I kept thinking of those slugs in my mother's garden. Every summer you see them with their fat little disgusting bodies."

I laughed.

"But actually, they were tasty. I guess if you use enough garlic and butter, you can make dirt taste good."

"Never thought about it quite like that. But you're probably right."

We walked a block or two in the direction of her apartment. I asked if she wanted to stop at another bar for a nightcap.

"No, not really. You can help me finish the bottle of scotch I bought. Maybe even make a fire, I've got wood."

"Sounds great," I confessed and we turned a corner to the block where she lived.

She lived in a renovated stone Victorian. She rented the top floor apartment and it had a small deck on the narrow roof. The apartment was furnished with modern leather and chrome chairs she had bought at the Merchandise Mart using her professional discount. There were a few abstract paintings hung on the wall.

Alice saw me looking closely at the paintings. She told me about a high school friend who was now a fiber artist, living in rural Montana who made them. "She did them right after graduate school and finally got painting out of her system. These are her last two. Everything else she has made are gigantic wall hangings."

We spent an hour or two talking about not much of anything. When she refilled my scotch from the bottle in the kitchen, I kissed her, and she didn't resist me.

After a few minutes of intimacy in the kitchen, she refilled my drink. I did not really want it. I was past my limit with alcohol. We wandered back into the living room where she played light jazz on her stereo, and danced around the room.

When we finished, I moved toward where I had dropped my sport coat on the arm of the couch. I slipped it on quickly and prepared to leave.

"You can spend the night, if you want," she whispered with a half-smile.

"Alright, I will."

Within a month, I left my furnished closet and moved in with her. We became a couple. From that point on, everything about the city became new and exciting. It seemed we tried to do it all: galleries and museums, the symphony, the opera, jazz and rock clubs, and restaurants, one after another in a town with endless variety.

I worked at a small advertising agency after leaving one of the industry giants that had brought me to Chicago from Memphis. While in Memphis, I handled political races in the middle South. I helped elect the

4

governors of Tennessee and Mississippi. I left the large agency because of their cutthroat manner. Among its many misdeeds, they handled publicity and Capitol Hill lobbying for the murderous Argentine junta leaders of the late 1970s. These were the same people who threw dissidents out of airplanes.

In the big Chicago agency, a single event put a bad taste in my mouth. I had had enough. I reported to a man who had been brought in from New York where he had handled high profile corporate headquarters accounts like drug and food companies. Unilever was one of his clients as was Pfizer. He was a senior vice president of a large marketing and publicity concern and an ex-Navy officer. He had attended the Naval Academy and had been operations officer on two guided missile destroyers prowling the Pacific and Indian Oceans. Don Highwood was obviously intelligent and experienced. He had an easy-going small town Nebraska demeanor that people accepted as good. His one fatal flaw was alcohol. It was his undoing.

He left New York with nothing but rave reviews from the industry. No surreptitious stories followed him to Chicago. Yet, once here he was introduced to our largest business clients. A few downtown lunches with them proved his demise.

One of the directors of Abbott Laboratories, that did millions of dollars with the agency, had lunch with Don. It was sort of an introductory thing. It had gone seemingly well, so the president of our communications monolith later learned. However, the second and third lunch within the next two weeks had the opposite effect. A terse and threatening telephone call from the Abbott top executive to the agency president became an ultimatum. He said "Get rid of this guy, this lush, or you'll lose this account. We don't work with drunks."

Don was fired within two days. His past caught up with him at last. There had been issues at his former firm. Over the last few years, he went from being a star to a pariah. He was unable to control his drinking in a society where everybody drank. He was pushed out of New York but was given ample time to land on his feet. He still had that star aurora surrounding him. Hence, they welcomed him to Chicago with a big salary. He was a pharmaceutical genius who had guided the world's largest companies through rough waters and strengthened their bottom line.

He called me into his office and told me that he had been fired. He did not know why. He didn't believe two lunches had forced the hand of our largest client. He believed it was something else.

We had lunch and since I liked him, I served as a confident in the ensuing days. It was difficult. Over a Chinese dinner several nights later, he admitted he had been forced out of his earlier company. He said he had hit rock bottom when his wife left with his son. He realized that his drinking escalated out of control after his service in the war. That seemed to be the time the downward spiral had begun in earnest.

I didn't see him for another week. One night I decided to give him a call and after two or three rings, he answered. His voice was incoherent. He told me he couldn't go on any longer and he would end it.

"What do you mean, end it?" I asked him cautiously. I heard nothing over the phone except his heavy breath.

"Fuck it," he announced and hung up the phone.

I sat silent for maybe five minutes. Then, I left my building. I waved for a cab to take me ten blocks to his Lakeside apartment. Inside his lobby, I rang the apartment buzzer for half a minute. The situation required overt action, so I tracked down the building supervisor and explained it all to him.

"I don't know, this isn't my business," the stocky Hispanic let out in a sigh.

Out of patience, I raised my voice, "If this guy takes a bottle of pills and dies in the next ten minutes, it's on you. That's what I'll tell the cops and the papers."

His face reddened. He thought about the possibility of that happening. "Ok, let's go," he told me. "But I don't like it."

I shook my head in acknowledgement for his discomfort and we walked together to an open elevator. We got in and took it to the tenth floor. Don's apartment was no more than five steps from the elevator on the 10th floor. We walked to the front door and the building supervisor opened it quickly with the master key.

"It's yours from here," he said and turned toward the stairs. He didn't want to wait for the elevator for some reason.

I walked inside the one-bedroom apartment. It was furnished by the building as a part of the rent deal. Looking around it was mostly cheap ill-matched furniture. Don was stretched out on the couch. There was a half-empty bottle of vodka in his hand and an open bottle of white pills spilled out on the glass coffee table next to him.

"What the hell are you doing here?" he bellowed. I wrestled the vodka bottle from his hand. It didn't take much effort. Then I picked up the pills and looked at the bottle label. They were over-the-counter sleeping pills.

"Get out," he demanded. He tried to sit up but he fell and slid back prone on the couch.

"How many of these did you take? I asked, angrily.

He shook his head. "Ten maybe. Who gives a shit?"

"I do. I'm not going to let you play the asshole and kill yourself."

"Nobody gives a shit."

"You've got a ten-year-old son. Use your goddamn brain."

I found the telephone and dialed information. I was then transferred to a poison control line. I talked to a doctor, who asked me to read him the label of the pills.

"OK, here's what you need to do. Get your friend to the toilet and shove your hand down his throat until he throws up. You say he's too drunk to stop you, right?"

"He's too weak. I can do it even if he fights me."

"Good. Do it and you will save his life. Once that is done get him to the emergency room. I am on duty at Northwestern downtown. You can bring him here."

"Right," I said, "and thanks a lot, doctor."

"Do it when we hang up," the doctor ordered and the line was dead.

I dragged Don from the couch with him trying to punch me. I batted away his hand. I dragged him across the floor in a life-saving swimming hold I had learned in the military into his tiny bathroom. I held him tightly with one arm around his head. I opened his mouth, and stuck my fingers down his throat as far as I could until he gagged. Then he vomited. Ten minutes later, he was awake leaning against the bathroom wall, conscious, and able to speak.

7

"You're going to put water on your face and change clothes. Your shirt at least. Then we are going to the emergency room at Northwestern. A doctor's waiting to see you."

He half-heartedly shook his head, "Why bother, let me die."

"Not on my watch" and I got his shirt off and cleaned him up.

When the taxi stopped at the Northwestern emergency room downtown, I manhandled him out of the cab. I found the doctor I talked with and he admitted Don as a trauma patient. He was sent to a locked ward upstairs for attempted suicide cases. Then told me he would not be able to see visitors from the outside for three days. That was the hospital rule.

On the way back home in the taxi, I realized my clothes and hands smelled of vomit. Later, I must have taken an hour-long hot shower to quell my own heightened emotions. Once out of the shower, I poured myself a strong whiskey and sat in bed. My mind continuously replayed the bizarre evening and its ending.

The next day, I was called into the agency president's office. He gave me a dressing down on my behavior. It wasn't the fact I saved a man's life, but it was because I, a firm employee, was involved in an embarrassing situation.

"Abbott could hear about this. If they do, they will probably drop us for hiring suicidal drunks. You're on notice for this."

I had a few drinks and thought about what happened at the office. I told them that I was through the next day. I quit. I didn't give them a reason.

It took three weeks to find a new job. After enough telephone calls, I found another much smaller company who needed experienced new blood. I joined them. They were three blocks down Wacker Drive from my old company. I told Alice the whole story the first week we were together. I had hoped to give her some insight into who I was. I wanted to become less of a stranger.

"You're deep, I didn't know. Now I do," she said hugging me.

I saw Don about two weeks after the incident. He was still being treated for psychiatric issues at Northwestern. Treatment lasted a month and when he was released, I invited him out for dinner. We talked about everything except what had happened. He told me he was going back to

New York. He knew people there who remembered him as he once was. He had hoped they might hire him. After that last dinner, I never heard from him again.

******

Two months living with Alice quickly turned into two years. She thought it was time to marry. I put her off for another 18 months with deft denials and because of my earlier marriage trials. One night, she finally gave me an ultimatum.

She put her wine down after the first long sip, "I may love you to death. But if you don't marry me by Christmas, I'm leaving. You have time to think about it. By now you know what you don't like about me, and whether you can live with that, or not. That's all I have to say." With that, she added, "It doesn't require any discussion. You know the rules of the game." She gave me a disingenuous smile and summoned the waiter who was hesitatingly hovering. He sensed something ominous was about to happen by our body language and the looks on our faces.

"Does Claude have the truffle pate?" she asked politely, and he nodded.

"Every Friday, our regulars expect it."

"Wonderful. I'll have that."

When the food was served, we, or at least, I stumbled on what to talk about next. She did not.

"You'll do the right thing," she whispered. "And now, let me tell you about the drama on who's going to design the State of Illinois building. They are bringing in a consultant who teaches at Yale. I am one of his two assistants. How I hate that place."

As much as I feared another difficult marriage, I wanted to be with her. I convinced myself that this was the right person. The lightning that once struck would not repeat itself. Therefore, three weeks after that dinner at the Bakery restaurant, I told her to pick a date for the wedding. She chose her birthday on July 3.

We were married in a small ceremony at a nearby Episcopal church with her family, my daughter and a handful of friends in attendance. The minister, the Right Reverend Harold Reed officiated. Before the wedding, we had to have a conference in the church study to access our eligibility or fitness, I'm not certain which.

9

The wedding was scheduled three weeks away. With warm weather, we walked the ten minutes it took to the church. Inside the sanctuary we heard Reverend Reed moving about, and upon seeing us, he'd forgotten why we'd come. I gently reminded him.

"Oh yes, our little chat to see that we're all in agreement."

As we sat down in his crowded study, I launched into this defense of my haphazard church going and ended with me confessing that I was indeed a Christian.

"That's interesting. First, tell me a little bit about yourselves. Alice, that's right, isn't it. Why don't you start?"

Alice told him an abbreviated story of her life, her values, and ended by telling him she had great respect for the place of the church in society.

"Thank you, that's good to know. About your values? Tell me; are you ready to spend your life with this man?"

Alice smiled and said, "I am."

The rector laughed tossing his head back and added, "People say that Harold Reed will marry anyone. I imagine it's true. God's will.

"Will you need music? We can find an organist if you'd like."

I shook my head no, and Alice nodded her agreement.

"We'll conduct the service at six sharp. Do you have a best man, and who will give Alice away then?"

"My father will be here for that."

"Perfect," said the reverend, "though we don't have to do it if you don't want to. The same thing with the best man. It's traditional which of course you know."

"You said you came from a family of clergymen," he inquired. "You mentioned them. Episcopal?"

I laughed. "No, the younger cousin is a Presbyterian minister and the other a Baptist. The Baptist minister conducts services at a Methodist church with a congregation of about fifty in a nearby town as well. After he preaches to the Baptists. An eleven-thirty service as I recall. Lives in the Methodist church home which is a bit larger."

"Fascinating. I have never heard of that. Two different denominations."

"Same God," I added with sarcasm.

"Indeed, it is," the rector exclaimed with a soft laugh. With a nod, he rose slowly from his desk and walked us through the church to the door.

"Thank you, Father," I said shaking his soft meaty hand and Alice expressed her appreciation too, smiling profusely as we headed down the stone church steps.

******

I originally came to Chicago because I had grown tired of the insular and cloying feeling I experienced in Memphis. Part of the reason for this feeling was the dependence my ex-wife had on her family and close friends and how it affected me. Her parents were nice, decent people, but being thrown together all the time bothered me. She was the problem. The marriage was a mistake from the beginning. A mistake made from infatuation. Had I looked closer and taken the full measure of my ex-wife's dysfunction, I would have stepped back and seen the train coming. It was easily predictable.

One morning, I flew to Chicago and interviewed at a large agency. I was able to do so without drawing undue attention at the Memphis office or with the family. The agency had lost a staffer with similar experience and offered me a generous salary. They hired me on the spot.

That meant I had entered the big time. I would live in one of the largest cities in the country. I did not know a soul there. They put me up at their expense at a downtown hotel for the first two months. Within that time, I was expected to find housing in the city or in one of the surrounding suburban towns. They were numerous and went on for miles in every direction except the east that was Lake Michigan.

I talked with Nancy about moving and she immediately refused. She would not leave Memphis for any reason. My doubled salary was not enough. Even the prospect of advancement with major players in my industry did not make a difference. My career meant nothing to her.

I hoped to discuss moving calmly and suggested we visit the city together. I would let her see whether something about it appealed to her, its differences, or simply the adventuresome nature of the prospect.

I had already accepted the job, and they gave me a date when they would expect me to show up for work. I had two weeks to familiarize myself with the city and introduce whatever family I had left to Chicago. There were shouting matches for days at a time until the weekend we boarded the plane for Chicago. The warm summer weather did not make it more appealing, and she made it clear she did not like the place.

She agreed that she would come for a month. So, I rented a picturesque apartment in a Greystone in upscale Lincoln Park. She flew back to Memphis at the end of the month. The next night she called me to tell me two things. The first was that she was not coming to Chicago and secondly, she wanted a divorce. That was how quickly our marriage ended.

The next week I received a letter from her lawyer that informed me that he had filled a motion for a divorce with the court. Tennessee recently passed a No-Fault Divorce law, so neither party had to prove malicious intent. Incompatibility was enough. He said that if I signed the enclosed court document, the next step would be the notification from the court of the actual divorce decree. We had agreed on child support while this was in progress. She would continue to live in the Memphis house her father owned, although we paid the mortgage. It was rather simple and abrupt. Now it felt I was floating on a piece of ice alone on Lake Michigan. Money would be tight.

The first place in Chicago I rented was a furnished bedroom with a communal toilet down the hall. The next joint at least had a Pullman kitchen with half again as much room. Quickly I learned about the world of a divorced man. The advantage I had was that I was just thirty.

I looked like every other single professional man to the eye. I was suited-up, had a decent haircut, youthful face, and good shoes. I could meet women in bars and I did. I appeared to be like everyone else. There were secretaries, shop girls, nurses and lawyers around. You just had to convince them you were worth the effort, through your looks and glib conversation. I could convince them, and sometimes did, with success. If one-nighters are considered productive. Mostly I was unhappy and lonely.

For a while, I spent time with a commercial artist, Wendy. In the evenings, we would drink cheap wine and she would draw me nude using charcoal. Her apartment was more comfortable than mine was, so we would usually go there after a dinner of cheap Mexican or Chinese food. Wendy had just graduated from Moore art school in Philadelphia. The ten-year difference in ages did not help the relationship. We often found ourselves at odds over things that would not matter to anyone else closer in age such as books, music, or the everyday occurrences.

During the six months we were a couple, she created a couple of portraits of me that were quite breath taking. I managed to keep one after it all ended. I once posed for a full-length nude drawing for her. The duration of the pose almost killed me. I felt an exhaustion I had never experienced before. She kept the drawing in her fine art portfolio. If it were still around today, I would love to have it.

I once took Wendy to an advertising agency dinner for middle level executives and wives. She had dressed like a Woodstock hippy for the event. I could see the eyes of the women examine her with distain. Fortunately, she was too young to sense it and consequently was not hurt. Her table conversation exonerated her because with art she could both perform and talk for hours with vast knowledge

I remember one of the agency wives at dinner, ten of us around a table, ask, do you ever work from a model?

"Yeah," Wendy said with a sort of bored air, while she picked at her Crème Brulé.

"Mostly I do nudes of him. But if your husband would like to pose, that's OK." The husband spat his mouthful of coffee into the air at the comment and his face reddened. Then he laughed and the rest of the table joined the mirth. From the corner of my eye, I could see the agency president shake his head slightly in disapproval at the conversation. The rest of the night was cordial. Most of the crowd treated Wendy as this sort of rebellious teenager.

There was dancing after dinner. Wendy studied interpretive dance one summer in New York during college. On the dance floor, she would break into odd arm-swinging movements with me during slow songs. I caught the disapproving glare from the agency head again. His look said, "What the hell do you think you're doing with that nutcase?" It was an evening to remember at the Palmer House. It certainly did not help my career.

The relationship, if you could call it that, with Wendy ended quickly. I think the age difference worked to kill us after the initial ardor cooled. She wasn't interested in talking about my daughter. But then, I was always circumspect about the subject. I also did not talk about my experience of a bad marriage either.

******

During the time with Wendy, I returned to Memphis for a short visit to see my daughter at the small house we had all lived in together. We had a quick fast-food lunch, I took her home, and I said my good-byes. Admittedly, I had been curt with my ex-wife who could not hide her disdain for me. We parted with harsh words.

As I walked down the gravel driveway to my rental car on the street in my slacks and sport coat, I heard frantic footsteps. As I attempted to turn around, Nancy threw a bucket of water on me. My clothes were literally soaked. Shocked and momentarily furious, all I could do was laugh. She then attempted to kick me, which I deflected. I left the madness behind me, mercifully, because I once had accepted it as my prison sentence.

Life in Memphis was a monotonous routine. It was every weekend with my ex-wife's parents at their lake house an hour away. It was pleasant enough and they were cordial except for their dominant presence in our lives. If Nancy needed money for some reason, clothing or furniture, she went to her father rather than discuss how we might afford it. There was something emasculating about it all. There was no option for me to look for a job in another city. I was stuck there. She went off birth control pills without bothering to tell me. My daughter's arrival came at a time where we were barely solvent in those days.

I think the reason I applied for a job in Chicago was an effort for some kind of independence. Although the allure of a real metropolis certainly was seductive. If I were to be honest, I would say by the end of the first year of marriage I had known I made a horrendous mistake. The pregnancy came along shortly after. At that point, I considered myself washed up. There seemed little I could do. I had no escape. I had little money and I did not have a reputation in the industry to fall back upon.

Life flattened out. I had a job with colleagues I liked and a modest livable home provided by my father-in-law. There were dinner invitations and friends but they were all hers. There was even a vacation home. She might have been dysfunctional then in those days, but she was not crazy. That would come later.

******

While in Chicago, I worked downtown in the advertising business like a thousand other guys. I lived in mean apartments and pinched pennies to support my daughter. It was bearable. There were demands like private kindergartens. Nancy wanted to put Sally on the wait list for an expensive Episcopal girl's school where she and her younger sister went.

Then, my former father-in-law suddenly sold the small house. My ex-wife and daughter temporarily moved in with her parents. It must have been about money though nobody bothered to explain why. In less than a year afterward, they moved to a cottage rental down the street from her parents.

By this time, I had met Alice and after living together in her small apartment, we moved to a handsome townhouse near DePaul University. It was spacious and grand to me and we had a guest room for the times Sally might visit.

I had left the large agency and after several years in partnership in another group, I decided to form a consulting company. I was able to acquire corporate clients quickly. Life was good or so I figured. One Saturday as I was working on some contracts I had brought home, the telephone rang.

The voice on the other end was my ex-wife's sister, "Do you know what's going on down here?"

My first thought was that my daughter had been in an accident or there was a serious illness requiring them to involve me.

"No," I answered, "I don't know what you mean."

"It's Sally," she continued.

"What's happened to Sally? I hope to God she's not hurt."

"That's not it, she's fine. But there is a problem that needs your attention. As her father."

15

"What?" I asked.

"You know Nancy's living in a cottage down the street, right?"

"Yeah. So, what's wrong?"

"What's wrong is Sally's decided she wants to live with my parents. She is over there weeks at a time doing whatever she wants. When I mention something about it and how it wasn't normal for the child, mother bites my head off. She told me to mind my own business."

At this point, her husband Robert came on the line. "It's not healthy. A child can't choose someone who lets them do whatever they want. It is going to mess her up. You'd better get down here. You're her father. Joyce and Tucker can't take in a grandchild just because they want to. It's against the goddamn law."

"Alright, I'll be down on Friday. Do you want me to call Joyce and Tucker?"

Robert answered, "Yes, you'd better do it now, tonight. Tell them you want to talk about Sally."

The sister added, "Something is way off in Nancy's head. She told me that Joyce could raise Sally. It didn't matter to her."

"I'll call Tucker and Joyce tonight. Tell them I want to meet on Friday. Maybe I should call Nancy first."

"Don't bother, unless you want a screaming match," the sister advised.

After hanging up, I made myself a scotch and sat on the couch. I stared blankly out the large windows onto the leafy street.

"This won't be pretty," I said to no one, and took a deep slug of the bitter liquid that stung my tongue.

I thought I would wait later to call the in-laws but, I could not think about anything else. I got the number from information and dialed it. Joyce answered the phone. I told her that I would be in town on Friday afternoon and that I wanted to meet with her and her husband. The subject was Sally.

"There's no need for us to talk, really," she said, a slight tinge of anger under the words. "Sally's fine with us."

"Sally should live with her parents, at least one of them. I'm sure you're loving grandparents, and I'm thankful for that. But no."

"Honestly, Sally is best with us."

"Unfortunately, it doesn't work that way. If your daughter can't take care of Sally, I will."

"Do you have enough room?" she asked condescendingly.

"Yes. I live in a beautiful three-bedroom townhouse in a lovely part of Chicago."

"Oh then, that's something new from the rented room."

"I've been here six months with a lady I'm engaged to, an architect."

"That's nice. But what about decent schools?"

"People go to schools here and go on to college. Joyce, don't be difficult."

She laughed. "Sally would be perfectly happy living with us. And she wants to. Taking her to Chicago would scar her."

"Joyce, if you and Tucker won't meet with me on Friday. We will do it another way. I'll get a Memphis lawyer and start custody proceedings. If your daughter is having issues with motherhood, I'm sure a courtroom will not help her. I'm asking you because you really are nice people and we can work this out if we talk."

There was a marked change in her voice, a business-like tone, flat and precise "If we must, alright. I will talk to Tucker this evening and we will meet you at the house on Friday, seven o' clock."

"I'll plan to see the two of you then," I added. "Goodbye."

"Yes," she answered, hanging up the phone.

I flew to Memphis that Friday and rented a car. I was going to be in their neighborhood a bit early, so I stopped at a café for a coffee. I had some time to reflect about what I was about to embark upon. Would they put up a fight? Would they tell me they would see me in court along with their daughter in a courtroom dispute? Maybe. Nancy's sister all but admitted there was something seriously wrong with Nancy's behavior. I suspected the parents knew this as well, but I doubt they would admit it.

It seemed my daughter's grandparents had completely taken over her life. She lived in their house. Her bedroom closet was full of school clothes and Joyce drove her to the Episcopal girls' school each day. The school I paid for.

Knowing I was financially strapped would they seek to make this a battle that would require high-priced legal fees? I might ultimately lose in

17

their hometown where they had many connections. Might they find a sympathetic judge to hear the case? Could they manipulate the system by knowing an insider? Could I bring my daughter to Chicago, probably against her will, since she had chosen to live with her grandparents? What would Alice say? Would she agree?

I sat at a luncheon counter and continuously stirred my coffee. I was nervously pondering my fate. I glanced at my wristwatch and figured that fate would be decided within the next twenty or thirty minutes.

It seemed like no time had passed and I was on the doorstep of my in-law's home. I rang the bell and Joyce greeted me with a forced a smile and said, "It's nice to see you. Come in."

She took me through the living room into the dining room where her husband sat at the long wooden table. He smiled even less convincingly than his wife did. I sat down and immediately started to speak. I said their youngest daughter and her husband had asked me to come down here because they were concerned about the neglect of my daughter.

"Why would she do that?" the father said. As he spoke, the corners of his mouth seemed to drop in obvious disapproval.

"This is none of her concern," Joyce quickly added.

"She's very comfortable here, with us," her husband exclaimed.

"I don't doubt that." I said, "But I'm her father and this is my responsibility. It's not yours to assume, though I know you've done that out of kindness."

"She's better off," Joyce quickly interjected. "I can take care of her, get her to school. If you ask her which you should, do you want to stay here? She'll answer yes."

"You can't act without my consent, I'm her father. It is time she's with me. I'll arrange it. I have a nice city home, and I'll get her into a good school."

"We don't agree," Joyce said.

"Joyce, you don't want us in a custody hearing in court. Not where my attorney calls your daughter an unfit mother or puts your younger daughter on the stand to testify against her sister. That would be madness. I don't want it."

Her husband spoke up: "Well, what is it you want to do? Why are you here?"

My mind was racing. I had not prepared a plan or anything to say. Nervously I cleared my throat and began to speak. "Your daughter and I can share custody like normal rational people. I will have several years with her in Chicago. She can come here summers to stay with you or Nancy, or both. Five years perhaps. That would make her sixteen and a junior in high school. She can spend her last year with you before college."

Joyce let out a sigh, and tears started to well up in her eyes. She touched them quickly with a handkerchief that was balled up in her fist.

"Let's avoid nastiness. Everybody loves her, let's express that, alright."

"Give us a couple of days to talk this over, and we'll call you," Tucker stated.

I stood up from the table and nodded to them both in acknowledgement.

"If you don't mind, I'll pick her up at school. We'll have a milkshake somewhere and visit for and an hour or so, and then I'll bring her back. I'm flying out at six."

I believed the way to sort this out was first to get their agreement. Then they would talk to Nancy whether she cared or not what might happen.

Joyce reminded me as I walked toward their front door that her younger daughter and her husband had no business calling me. They shouldn't have begged me to come down here to fix something that didn't need repair. It didn't concern them.

"I'm going to talk to Jeanie about this. She went way beyond her place. Things were fine as they were."

"You'll call me tomorrow evening, right?" I said to her as I was about to start down the front stone steps to the sidewalk. She didn't answer me but nodded, and the closed the door.

It was a five-minute drive to the school, and I got into line with the other cars, which were there to pick up their children. When my turn came, I got out of the car and waved to Sally who came running toward me as soon as she saw me. I told the teacher who I was, and flashed a driver's license for identification, and she thanked me.

19

Sally wanted to go to McDonald for their fake ice cream so that's where we went. I remembered there was one on Southern Avenue near the university. We sat outside in the fall sunshine, and talked, or rather she did. She was excited to tell me everything about school, and her pony Possum at Rachel Johnson's Barn in Germantown.

Anxious to start the process of her living with me, I said, "I talked with Joyce and Tucker, and we agreed that maybe you should go to school in Chicago and live with me. Wouldn't you like that?"

Sally had a pouty look on her face. She stared down at the ground. "I don't have any friends there. I don't know anybody. I want to stay with Joyce."

"It would be for a little while, and you'll make friends. And in the summer, you can come back here and stay with Joyce or your mother."

In quick response, Sally shook her head no. "I don't want to stay with you or my mother; I want to stay with Joyce."

I sighed at the exchange, and I figured there was little I could do to persuade a childlike Sally. She had only known a single place as home. She also had an attraction to her pony that I bought. There would be some difficulty in making this all happen.

I took her back to Joyce and Tucker, and we said our goodbyes. I was back in Chicago within three hours. All I had to do now was to wait for the telephone call to know where I stood.

At six sharp the next evening, Joyce called me with Tucker on the extension and sounded very businesslike in her manner.

"We discussed this last night. This is what we are prepared to do. We recognize you are Sally's father and have legal rights and responsibilities for your daughter. Tucker has suggested that we have Sally live with you in Chicago first for a two-year period, starting this coming end of summer. For the school year. In the summer, she would return to Memphis for two months. If that's ok, we can avoid lawyers and courts. We know that our position as guardians would be difficult to establish; in court, I mean."

I felt a rush of euphoria pass through my body after she finished. "That's agreeable to me. My feeling is that she will spend maybe three years here, and she can spend her last year before college in Memphis. With either you or her mother."

"Yes," Joyce said, but there was no mention of her daughter. She didn't mention anything regarding Nancy's opinion on the proposal. I knew that there was no point in me calling Nancy to discuss the conversations. I would be subjected to screaming fits.

"I would like to come up and visit your house first and meet your fiancée. Is that possible?" Joyce asked.

I told her it was, and we would welcome her.

"Are there appropriate schools there, private perhaps, where you might send her?"

That comment made my blood boil, but I remained calm, answering, "There's one I have in mind, at the University of Chicago, yes. It's a famous school."

We agreed that I would come down to Memphis the beginning of August and return to Chicago with Sally. They would plan a visit around September 15th. They wanted to see my living situation and the suitability of my townhouse. They also wanted to know what I had done about a school. The whole agreement seemed a bit pretentious and out of line on their part and it was. However, I was determined to make it all work outside of a courtroom.

Male friends counseled me to go into court and take care of it once and for all. This came from men who had experienced nastiness after a divorce with an unreasonable ex-spouse. They had tried to work things out like custody and child support payments, and suddenly minds were changed, and behavior became unhinged. Still, I thought my way would be the best for Sally, Alice, and myself. It would be civil and cooperative despite the hurt feelings in Memphis. For some reason, Nancy remained silent. She let her parents make arrangements for Sally, to which I agreed.

Eighth grade tuition at the University of Chicago Laboratory School was five thousand dollars. For that princely sum in my eyes as a product of coal town public schools, Sally would attend one of the most lauded secondary schools in the entire country with a rich history of progressive education going back to 1890.

I had launched my consulting company, and I would triple my earlier salary by the end of the year. Also, there was the money that Alice brought in as an architect. Yes, we could cover the tuition.

For some unknown reason, Joyce came alone. She booked a room at the downtown Drake Hotel for two days if necessary. After hotel check-in, she took a taxi to our townhouse. We greeted her for drinks and a house tour. This was the first time she met Alice. She had known little about her except what I said in Memphis.

Following a cocktail, we walked the two blocks to a French Bistro where we were known and had dinner and talked for almost two hours. There were questions about how this would play out since Alice, and I worked. We explained our plan for school and life at home.

"Is this place safe?" Joyce asked looking out the window at a busy commercial street with noise and people.

"Yes, it is," Alice, responded. "We would never do anything that might harm Sally."

I could see that Alice was trying her best to be agreeable to Joyce, and wanted to allay whatever fears the woman might have.

"It's so crowded in this city, where do children play?" Joyce said in a flat voice.

Alice took a breath and said, "That's a bit more complicated. My friends with children arrange for the kids to socialize through the school, or outside activities, like ballet or competitive swimming. These people are very careful about everything. They realize we live in one of the largest cities in this country."

"You go to someone's house, or to a school event then," Joyce stated.

I added, "Joyce, hardly anyone Sally's age plays on the street in Memphis. Either in your neighborhood or Nancy's."

"I'm aware of that. I was simply asking."

Now I was pretty much out of patience. I explained to her that we had friends with children Sally's age, and we would seek to introduce her to their kids. After we finished the thornier part of the conversation and the meal, I arranged for a taxi to return Joyce to her hotel.

Outside before she got into the cab, I explained, "I'll meet you at the hotel lobby at eight thirty tomorrow morning. We have a meeting at nine fifteen with the Lab School headmaster, and she'll give you a tour of the school."

"That's good," Joyce said,

"Oh, there's one other thing. Sally will have to take an entrance exam for admission; it is a university thing. I imagine she'll have no trouble passing it."

"I would think not," Joyce responded. "She goes to St. Mary's."

"This is the University of Chicago. They think of themselves in the league with Yale and Harvard."

After hearing that, she turned her back and went inside the revolving doors. I did not see her when I entered the hotel lobby at eight twenty the next morning. I was irked. Though it was not long before the elevator door opened, and she appeared.

The university campus was very gothic looking with buildings created to mimic those at Oxford or Cambridge. The Laboratory School had its own stone building with gargoyles on the roof. Inside everything was dark wood and stained glass. We strolled down the hall in search of the headmaster's office,

"This is a rather gloomy place; I don't think I'd want to go to school here."

"It's a top school, and that's the architecture style they've chosen."

Inside the anteroom, we waited a few minutes before we were ushered into the headmaster's office. The headmaster was a woman who resembled an older version of the singer and actress Bette Midler.

She sang the praises of the school, and its vaunted past, and the success in life of its many students which included scholars, scientists and top government officials. After her preamble, we walked the halls, and she opened a classroom door with students, which reminded me of a college class.

"Our students are challenged intellectually," she said. "And we don't apologize for that. We expect rigor and discipline, and curiosity from them."

As I stood next to the headmaster, I could see her large teeth and smelled the very strong perfume she wore. Joyce remained silent for the entire tour. Finally, she led us to the front door and handed me a paper with the times when the school entrance exams would be held.

"When your daughter finishes with her exam, I will ask the proctor to bring her to my office where we might have an interview. This

23

will give me a feeling of her interests and personality so we can better serve her."

We shook hands and I called a taxi, which came within two minutes to take Joyce back to her hotel and me home. In the taxi, Joyce let out this sigh. "They're very proud of their intellectual reputation. But the place gives me the creeps. It doesn't seem to be a place Sally might like."

Fed up with Joyce's pretension, I still held my temper, "She makes friends easily and it will stimulate her, I'm sure. I'd love to go to school there."

"I'm sure you would."

Not much in way of conversation took place for the ride up Lake Shore Drive and along the big lake to the hotel. When we stopped in front of the Drake, Joyce said, "There's no reason for me to stay any longer. You kept your word. Tucker has talked to Sally and convinced her that this is the right thing to do. Spend a few years with your father. She'll be ready to leave Memphis the end of August."

I nodded and added, "The headmaster said the entrance exams were the week of August twentieth. School starts after Labor Day. Oh well, I'm sure things will work out. Goodbye."

I got out of the taxi, walked her to the door, and watched her disappear into the hotel.

As we got closer to the end of the summer, Joyce said that it was a better idea if she just put Sally on a flight to Chicago alone. I could meet her at the airport. For several weeks, they had talked to her convincing her that the period she would spend away from them would be brief, at least that was their logic. They reassured her that summers would come by quickly and she would be with them again, at home, her true home.

I had to overcome that mindset that they instilled in Sally. I reckoned it was better than the outcome of an acrimonious court case with shouting and crying. Vile things, including lies, are always said in support of your case. They would work on tearing me apart. They would examine my failures whatever they were, true or not, in painful excruciating detail.

I also had to consider Alice in these plans. I asked her if she was comfortable with this. She told me since we would soon be married it came with the territory. She liked Sally and we would create a city family like the women at her architectural firm and others we knew.

Alice had a work friend with an adopted daughter who was a junior at the University of Chicago School. Her daughter drove to Hyde Park from our neighborhood every day. To encourage a friendship, Alice invited the family over for dinner. We talked about the possibility of Sally joined her in the morning. For her help, we would pay for gas and that seemed to please everyone.

On a Sunday afternoon then in mid-August, Sally flew into O'Hare. I met her at the gate, and we drove to the townhouse. Curious with the city and its bustle, she looked out of the window for most of the trip to the DePaul neighborhood mostly silent. Half-nervous about her arrival, I chattered about a variety of topics of which I had little interest, only to create a relaxed atmosphere for the drive.

"You don't know how good it makes me feel to have you live with me, with us. It makes me so happy."

She said, softly, "Un-huh," and continued to look out the window.

"There's one thing we have do though, tomorrow. We need to go to the school, and you'll have to take an admissions test. They want to know what you learned at St. Mary's."

"I don't think I learned anything," Sally said, this time turning to look at me.

"Sure, you did. That's a very good school, and they take education seriously."

"If you say so," Sally said disinterested.

At home, I found a parking space in front of the house and emptied the trunk with her two suitcases. Inside Alice had made a beautiful dinner. There were flowers and lit candles on the dining room table to announce Sally's arrival.

After putting the suitcases in her bedroom upstairs and showing Sally around the house, we all sat down to a dinner of chicken breasts and brown rice and asparagus. Alice was good at keeping the conversation light and yet lively as she sensed subjects that might interest Sally who seemed resigned to being here.

"Is this school I'm going to going to be hard? Grammy said it might. That it was part of a big college."

I quickly added, "You're a smart girl, and St. Mary's prepared you just fine. Don't worry. There's only a test they make everybody take, and you'll ace it tomorrow."

Sally shook her head. "I hate tests, always have. They make me nervous."

Now Alice spoke: "Oh, this is so they know about everything you learned in Memphis. You went to a great school down there. It won't be a problem."

"If you say so," Sally added.

She smiled, and said in a gentle manner, "Alice, you're a very good cook. The chicken is delicious."

When she said that I could see a light in Alice's eyes, which were filling with tears of joy, these first obstacles overcome.

"Maybe you can teach me to cook while I'm here," Sally said. "My grandmother never had the time."

"I'd love to. I come from an Italian family and wonderful dishes were an important part of my life. My Osso Buco is restaurant quality."

"What's that?" Sally inquired.

"Veal Shanks."

"Oh, I see," muttered Sally shrugging her shoulders.

"We have a German butcher shop in the neighborhood. It has been here a hundred years, and they have fabulous meats. I'll teach you how to make all the classic Italian dishes.

"Sounds like fun," Sally said tossing her dirty blond hair to one side.

When the time for The University of Chicago admissions test came, I held my breath after the forty-five-minute session. I had no idea how she might do. I had only talked to her Memphis teachers a few times since I had lived in Chicago, and they didn't offer much. They said that she was doing fine but who knows what that could mean.

Proctors graded the test in the room within fifteen minutes. It wasn't long before the headmaster appeared in the hallway to talk to gaggles of anxious parents. When she got to us, she smiled and said, "Sally will be a great addition to our student body. We don't have any Southerners. She's a smart girl."

26

Sally was accepted as a student, and now we would need to prepare with clothes, and everything else she would need for a new school. I drove her to school her first day and met a few of the parents of classmates in front of the gothic building. Half of the school were children of professors, and the other half was made up from Hyde Park and other areas of Chicago.

Two weeks went by, and Alice's friend's daughter stopped each morning in front of the house to pick her up for school. I gave her a week's worth of gas money. Sally made friends readily and her classmates liked her strange accent, and it made her special.

One night I got a call from Memphis, it was Nancy, Sally's mother. She said that it was necessary for her to fly up and see her daughter's situation if this arrangement was going to work. I listened patiently to her rambling explanation and told her to come whenever she liked.

She arrived that Friday morning after Sally had gone to school. I drove her down to Hyde Park and took her around the school grounds. What I knew of them. We had a coke in the school cafeteria, sitting among the students, and her eyes seemed to take in the room.

"This place is a like a prison," she said, "so dark and menacing."

"It's part of a great university."

Nancy snorted, "Well, I wouldn't want to be here. St. Mary's was full of light and green lawns."

"Sally will prosper here, I know it."

Now she shook her head, "I don't think so. I've seen enough, let's go."

"Would you like to speak with the headmaster, she's quite nice."

"No, I just want to leave."

I drove home making whatever civil conversation I could, and in front of the house, she stood and stared at it and the other houses down the street.

"A whole block of Victorians, reminds me of Boston."

Inside the house, she met Alice who had left work early. We had a cocktail, sat in the living room and talked. Toward the end of the conversation, the door opened, and Sally came in carrying a backpack. She started up the stairs.

"Sally," Nancy called out and she ran over to embrace her mother.
"You made it. Do you like Chicago?" Sally asked.

"It's very busy," Nancy managed to blurt out.

I said, "Sally, Alice and I are taking your mother to the French bistro for dinner. Do you want to join us?"

"Nah thanks. I've got too much to do. You can talk like adults without me there." With that, she waved at her mother and started up the stairs to her bedroom.

"This is very different for her. I hope it has a happy ending."

Her sarcasm irritated me. Alice was probably irritated as well though she gave no indication of her displeasure. We got up and walked the three blocks to the restaurant. The French owner Marcel greeted us with enthusiasm. "So, this is little Sally's mother. Yes, I can see the resemblance especially in the beautiful eyes."

"Madam, Monsieur, please follow me to your favorite table. You are early enough, voila."

After the fanfare, we ordered. Nancy ordered in French since she had minored French in college. Marcel replied in kind.

The table conversation was mostly amicable. It was difficult to see behind Nancy's half smile, so I didn't bother. She didn't like the situation, yet she was afraid to push back against her parents. It was an agreement everybody signed off on, like an armistice. There appeared to be no reason for fighting amongst families, and I sensed that Nancy accepted this in her grudging way.

She wasn't speaking to her younger sister who initiated this though I reckoned that would somehow resolve itself before too long.

"Jeanie had no business calling you," she finally said at the table.

"She told me she did it out of concern for Sally," I answered.

"Didn't like Joyce taking over Sally's upbringing.'

"It didn't happen that way."

"Well, it is where it is. Sally appears to be happy. I know I am. I can find no fault with spending more time with my own daughter. She's connected to both families."

Alice tried to change the conversation, but Nancy persisted. I didn't back down.

28

I said, "You're entitled to your beliefs in how you see the world and the present circumstances. I'm convinced they have changed for the better. It's important for Sally to have the benefit of a father around her every day. Not as a visitor."

"You came to Chicago; you didn't have to. It's your fault."

"Let's be civil if we can. What is done is done. It's now about Sally, ok?" I uttered, perhaps more forcefully than I meant to. "It's late and I have an early morning client meeting. So, if you don't mind, let's call it an evening. You can say goodnight to Sally, and I'll take you back to the hotel."

She stood up and said, "Let's get this over with." We left the restaurant. As I opened the front door, I caught Marcel's eyes, and with a frown, he shook his head in empathy.

Once she had gone back to whatever she had in Memphis, our life in the townhouse went back to normal. Alice was off to work at the architects in the morning. Sally went to the Lab School, which kept her busy, and I went to an office with a British friend and business partner consulting with large industrial concerns.

Every evening, we would have a sit-down dinner in the dining alcove we created off the townhouse large living room. It brought the three of us together. It would usually become a forum of what we'd done during the day or had planned for later. Sally had attracted a handful of girlfriends already, her newness in the class and Southern accent helped make her special to others.

We were invited to the homes of Alice's friends who had children her age. Sally managed to strike up a friendship with Alice's immediate boss's daughter after a few dinner invitations. They lived in a close-in Chicago suburb. We would have dinner every other month and visit for Easter and join them for mass.

The integration of Sally into my life again came without strain. After the first few months of nightly telephone calls with Joyce, she acted like every other child with a nuclear family. She was always cooperative with Alice and treated her as mother substitute perhaps closer in relationship to her grandmother Joyce rather than her mother.

As far as I was aware, there were no nightly telephone calls to her mother. Those to Joyce ended after several months. Sally needed friends of course at school, and luckily, she had made them. I learned that her teachers liked her, as she was a willing and able student. She would wear an old string of pearls Joyce had given her to class several days a week. Mary Robinson, who was her homeroom and English teacher, called her "Pearly." The transition could have been difficult in this radical new environment with Alice and me but, it seemed seamless.

Consequently, we started to take on the appearance of a cohesive family. We would do things together spontaneously like eating dinner every Wednesday night at a tiny Mexican restaurant nestled under the Elevated train. Sally loved it for its tasty and plentiful beef tacos. Plus, we could get out of there for twenty dollars.

Sally blossomed and her circle of friends widened. It was not long before she was invited to spend weekends staying over at the professors' kids' houses in Hyde Park. We may have seen her less, but her teenage life was rich with many friends. Occasionally we would have a classmate spend the night at our townhouse however most of the school social life centered on the Southside university neighborhood.

Around this time, Alice had come to the end of her patience with her architecture firm and with the profession as well. We would talk after Sally left the dinner table and she told me she wanted to quit architecture. She would pursue a creative writing career, books or magazines maybe. She needed to be in a writing community, needed to learn the basic skills. She believed a graduate degree would solve all those issues and she could do it in Chicago. Two universities here had degree programs in that discipline. She figured they would take her on as professional, changing careers. She'd written tons of construction and design reports during the past ten years. She had already taken the initiative contacting the University of Illinois that had a journalism master's program and was keen to populate it with students. By the time we finally talked about it, she already had two interviews. The professors she had spoken with reported they didn't see any problem with her starting in September, which was three months away.

When Sally's school term ended, I honored the agreement I had reached with Joyce and Tucker, and I sent her back to Memphis for the balance of the summer. She would return to Chicago two weeks before school began, which was right after Labor Day.

30

Alice took the plunge. She shocked her architecture firm that she was not only leaving them after ten years but the whole profession itself. Within two weeks, she had set up a writing space for herself in the back bedroom, which faced the El tracks.

She started her writing by doing a historical architecture article for Chicago magazine on the classical downtown buildings of the 1920s. I asked her how in the world she gotten them interested in running the article. Alice told me she picked up the telephone and called the editor who happened to be looking for a feature for an upcoming issue. It was pure luck, she told me. Otherwise, she busied herself preparing for university classes. She read a lot, mostly contemporary authors and a few of the greats.

It wasn't long before Sally was in the Chicago house again readying herself for the new school year. One night before classes, one of her school friends came over for a Saturday night stay. I could hear them talking schoolgirl gossip well into the night.

With everybody in class, I started to take more of an interest in cooking. I told Alice that I would be responsible for dinner every Saturday for the entire school year. Dinner would focus on seafood, since I had discovered the new Chicago Fish House, which supplied most of the upper Midwest with fresh fish.

At the dinner table that Saturday before school commenced, I announced quite formally that I had christened my endeavor as The Year of Cooking Fish. I was quick to add that every week would be different. I would never repeat the dishes, ever.

Sally's fish IQ was limited to shrimp, so I put that sea creature on the bottom of my list. I was determined to use the most exotic seafood I could locate and prepare it a classic fashion.

The Chicago Fish House was an institution that supplied ten thousand restaurants in Chicago and Detroit and everywhere in between. They had built a new building out North Avenue west of downtown. And it had a sizable retail store for customers, while truck after truck left the loading dock for regular restaurant delivery across the Midwest.

My first visit to the fish market was an eye-opener. I never seen so many seafood offerings in a single place. It was difficult to make any kind of rational decision. Then again, why be rational. Inside the case coiled on a bed of ice, I saw what looked like a small python, jet-black with a thick curved body. I asked the clerk what it was. He smiled, "Atlantic eel."

I cleared my throat and inquired further how to prepare the delicacy. He said, "Honestly, I don't know. But we have a French guy in the back who has had them a lot. I'll get him," and he disappeared through the swinging metal doors. A few seconds later, a mustached middle-aged man followed him through the open doors and came over to where I was standing.

"That is an excellent choice," he said with a broad smile. "I grew up in Normandy and we had them all the time." He turned and grabbed a piece of butcher paper and laid it on the case. "Here's what you do," and he began to write quickly in large legible cursive his family recipe for the eel. "You've never had anything as good," he noted, handing me the paper.

He learned closer toward me at the glass case and added, "Take pliers from your tool kit, and pull away the skin. Once you get a good grip, keep yanking, and it will come off like a snakeskin. Then you're ready to cook it." He uttered, *Bon Chance*, saluted me and was quickly gone.

The Atlantic eel would be the inaugural dish in my year of cooking. It would be a reconciliation with my young daughter and my life with Alice. I left the store with a bounce in my step. On the way to my car, I thought I make a quick trip to Sam's, the ancient wine store nearby to marry the eel with the right wine.

In truth, Sam's was a warehouse with a huge selection of vintage wines. Inside I found the owner, old gnarly Sam himself, and explained what I wanted. He motioned for me to follow him down these circular wrought iron steps into a kingdom of cardboard boxes filled with wine bottles. The only two signs I saw were France and California. Sam led me down the aisle into the French section where we made two sharp right turns, and he stopped seemingly out of breath.

"Here it is. This is what you need for the eel. A Rhone Valley wine that is very robust and known for its flavor. The vineyard is Hermitage. It a family of winemakers going back two hundred years."

He handed me a bottle, and I examined the label and wine color.

"How much?" I asked him, and he shook his head, saying, "Twenty-five bucks."

"A little pricey," I added without much thought.

"Well, you said this was for a family dinner, right?"

"Yes, for my daughter." I hesitated for a moment and added, "And wife."

Sam leaned closer to me, "Look I'm an old man. I only wish I had my wife and daughter to savor this wine. Don't waste your life."

With that, I agreed with him, and took two bottles to checkout. In the car, I knew I still had one more errand to run. I drove northward to Andersonville to a French bakery I knew and bought two large fresh baguettes.

Now I was ready and aimed the car homeward to begin my seafood journey. It would be a Normandy eel dish, cooked for hours in the crock-pot, ready for a succulent Saturday evening feast. I would begin cooking tomorrow morning when Alice was at the university in a seminar, and Sally returned from an overnight in Hyde Park.

Planning the cooking steps in my head, I would have the house and kitchen to myself. First, I needed pliers, and we didn't have one in the apartment toolbox that Alice brought with her.

There was a small hardware store on Webster three blocks away, so I walked there in the brisk autumn. At the hardware store, the clerk who was probably the owner asked me what I wanted. I told him a pair of pliers.

"What kind of pliers?" he asked impatiently though no one else was in the small store.

"Just piers," I answered curtly.

"Well, let me ask it a different way. What are you going to use them for?"

"To skin an Atlantic eel."

"Skin an eel?" he said thinking that I was half-crazy.

"It's like this. You grab some skin and keep pulling until it comes off. Like you were skinning a snake."

He shook his head, "I've never skinned a snake."

"Neither have I. But it must be similar."

"OK, enough with snakes. Follow me and I'll show you the pliers. You pick the one you think will do the skinning job."

The small half-crouched man led me to a display of pliers in the rear of the cramped store with squeaky floors.

"Is this a big snake or a small one?" he asked turning his head.

"It's an eel not a snake," I added.

"Well, why didn't you say that in the first place," he said smiling. "This ought to skin a two-foot eel, for sure." Then he handed me an ordinary looking pair of pliers."

I returned home before noon, and I began to examine the creature that I had bought. At first glance, I would swear it was water moccasin. It reminded me of a poisonous snake I once saw at my feet in a Mississippi cotton field. It had left my presence without extending any familiarities. But I still remember its thick black body and small head. It was very poisonous.

Putting a dishtowel on the kitchen counter, I laid the sea creature out for closer examination and felt its smooth body. It had no fishy smell, really no scent at all, it seemed. I figured it was two feet long from its narrow head to tail, with a thick serpentine body.

Nobody instructed me how I was to skin it properly. I had to trust my own instincts in the matter. I cut the eel below its head and extended the slice around the circumference of its body, not too deep but short of decapitation. With my newly purchased pliers, I readied myself for the skinning. I reckoned that if you had a strong grip on a piece of skin, you could easily tear it off, probably in a single motion.

Gripping a flap of skin firmly that I had cut near the eel's head, I started to pull but nothing seemed to happen. This is going to require manhandling, and I prepared myself to pull with all my strength. Making a Neanderthal loud grunt, I began to pull with the piers, but the eel bounced on the towel making it difficult to continue.

To solve that, I gripped the creature firmly with my free hand and pulled hard with the pliers. I could see the skin separate from the eel showing a whitish flesh. Now full of resolve, I started to pull in earnest while making guttural sounds.

At that moment, Sally stuck her head into the kitchen, and almost shouted, "Good God, what are you doing?"

"I'm…" I said with a half-prepared response.

"Why are you killing that snake? Did it attack you in the house?"

"It's our dinner."

"I'm not going to eat a snake, that's gross."

I told her it was not a snake but rather an Atlantic eel that I bought at the fish market, and I was preparing it for dinner.

"Count me out," she said. "I'll have a peanut butter sandwich."

I told her about the Frenchman at the fish market who'd given me his Normandy family recipe.

"This will be perfect, a real treat. Alice will love it."

As I said that Sally ran upstairs to the safety of her bedroom, determined not to have any visual contact with the expired sea creature. Oh well, I thought, if she had not seen it and waited for her plate that would be an entirely different story.

Finishing the skinning took another few minutes but it wasn't too hard. By this point, it was a sea creature with white flesh and a hidden backbone. I removed it, cut the two-foot eel into four-inch squares and put them aside. Next, I sautéed garlic cloves with butter also reserved for later.

I wrestled the crock-pot out of the cupboard and set it up on the counter, plugging it into the socket. I sliced a few carrots into bite size chunks and threw them into the pot along with peeled pearl onions I had bought. I added Yukon Gold baby potatoes plus the sautéed butter and garlic mixture. Then went in a package of seafood stock and a cup of water.

I slowly put the pieces of eel into the liquid until most of them were submerged. I uncorked the Hermitage Rhone Valley red wine, and generously put half the bottle into the pot, topping it off. Lastly, I added three sprigs of fresh rosemary and put on the lid. I placed the temperature on the high setting and looked at my watch calculating the three hours that it would need to cook.

This would be a one-dish fisherman's dinner, and we would have a steamy hot baguette for dipping in the broth. Within an hour, the kitchen and the downstairs began to smell like a Normandy fishing village in my mind. It would be a feast indeed.

The front door opened, and I heard Alice cry out, "What is that delicious smell? Fish glorious fish." She immediately started to dance around the living room once she had hung up her coat.

"How was the seminar?" I asked her with genuine curiosity.

"This degree is going to be more work than I once thought. They want a lot of writing out of me in a short time."

"You're smart, you can do it."

She smiled at me, "Enough of the school talk. What have you prepared?"

I stood tall, and announced, "Tonight you will dine on Atlantic eel in a Rhone Wine sauce, fresh off the boat, and cooked to perfection.

"Will you set the table while I finish up in here?" I asked.

"I will, Monsieur."

Once the bread was warmed, we were ready to eat. I put the eel concoction in a large bowl where we could comfortably serve ourselves.

"I'd like a scotch before we eat," she said to me in the kitchen. "How about you?"

"Nah," I said, a little miffed. "I have a bottle of Rhone for us."

She said, "Suit yourself; I'm not much of a wine drinker."

By this time, Sally was downstairs, and her face did not show much enthusiasm for the dinner.

"When I came in, he was cutting the poor creature's throat," she complained to Alice.

Hearing that in the kitchen, I answered I was skinning it.

Sally shook her head, "I can't begin to tell you how awful that sight was."

Alice finished her drink and laughed. "I've never eaten eel before, I'm excited."

Once the hot bread was on the table, I brought out the bowl with the eel and put it down in front of the seated women. I announced, "Voila."

Alice took a heaping bowl and two handfuls of bread. She put her spoon into the dish, sipping the liquid first, and exclaimed, "This is the best seafood I've ever had."

I filled my own bowl and put some into Sally's bowl that she just stared at for maybe a minute before trying a spoonful of the broth. "Not bad," she finally admitted.

Clearing my throat, I announced to Alice that for her entire time in graduate school, on Saturdays we would have fresh fish. I told her that this marathon of flavor, starting today was the beginning of The Year of Cooking Fish.

"Oh great, worse than this next week," Sally added rolling her eyes.

"I should let suspense take over, but I won't," I chortled. "I have talked with my fishmonger, and next week they're expecting a shipment of fresh Pompano from South Florida, where it's in season. Next Saturday's dinner will be pompano inside '*papillote*'. Which is white-fleshed fish cooked inside a parchment bag, where the butter and herbs will infuse the fish."

Sally said, "Can't we have hot dogs?"

"Absolutely not."

After dinner, I topped off my glass from the table with the rest of the Rhone bottle we saved for the eel and sat down in the living room.

"Is it cold enough for a fire tonight?" I asked Alice who was making herself another scotch.

"Nah. After this I'm going to bed, but I'll sit for a minute."

I asked her how the first few weeks of the master's program were going, and she shrugged her shoulders. "I don't honestly know. They have assigned me a five-thousand-word story, which is about ten pages on anything I want. It's too broad. I don't know what to write."

Shaking my head, I said, "Well, you complained about how bad architecture has gotten within the last eight or ten years, from the golden era. You can find architect friends to interview, who feel like you. Interview three of them maybe and express your opinions."

"Oh gawd, I wanted to get away from architecture," she complained.

"Write what you know, factual and with your individual style. Like Chicago Magazine commissioned it."

"But I want to get away from all that."

"Do it once and never repeat it."

She nodded in agreement and started up the stairs with her drink, which was a habit I didn't like. Yet I didn't want to be pushy.

During the next week, Alice threw herself into writing the article. Late at night, I could hear the computer keys click as she dove into her piece with abandon. On the second night at two am, I walked to the back bedroom. She was typing away with a glass of scotch on the table next to her notes.

"Time for bed," I said cheerfully.

"I'm almost there, another hour maybe."

"The liquor's going to make you pay big time tomorrow," I said, pointing at the drink.

She told me she could handle it, and smiled at me saying, "Goodnight, see you shortly."

Her paper or article on the current state of Chicago architecture got a top grade. It was the best in her small class because she was so knowledgeable about the profession, and a good writer to boot. This was only the first of intense writing assignments she would face up until Christmas. All designed to see who might be weaned out of her cohort of would-be journalists. If you were there, it was expected that you already knew how to write snappy prose that only required light editing.

Yet Alice agonized with every writing assignment. She was convinced in the back of her mind that she shouldn't be there and that she wasn't good enough. During an average week, she might be up all-night writing, downing a couple of scotches in the process.

Even when her major professor called her in and asked her to be his teaching assistant, sort of erasing her tuition, she balked. He wanted her to grade undergraduate essays and make relevant comments that he could speak to in class.

My pompano dinner had been a huge success; everyone loved the sweetness of the fish and the marrying of the three herbs I added.

Next up, was perhaps the most bizarre seafood choice. One Saturday I found skate wing tips, which came from rays. They are undulating paper-thin creatures who filled the ocean with a lethal stinger on its tail.

Cooking instructions came from the James Beard cookbook. It required a marinade with a soy sauce and honey, and then to lightly sauté it. You finished the dish with cream and capers. The cooking was similar in fashion to a veal Marsala that I'd mastered some time ago when I first started cooking. The secret to a dish of skate wings is not to overcook the thin pieces. Get them ready on a low heat and raise it to finish with capers and cream sauce.

For the dinner, I didn't bother to let Sally or Alice know what the fish was. I prepared a garden salad and brown rice to accompany the dish. Earlier we had bought a Japanese rice cooker so that made this step mindless. I whipped up a traditional French mustard vinaigrette for the greens.

I served the salad and as everyone remained seated. Then I finished the skate wings and presented them on a bed of rice with the cream and capers.

Sally was the first one to comment on the fish. "What is this anyway? It's luscious," she sang out.

"You've outdone yourself," Alice chimed in with a big smile on her face.

"It's skate, the tip of the sea ray's wings as they're called."

"Huh," said Sally,

"Those big rays that swim in the ocean. You cook the tips of their wings."

Sally exclaimed, "Things can only get weirder with your cooking."

There was no doubt that Alice was prospering at the university. One of her professors even suggested a doctorate and a path as an academic. However, that was not what she wanted. Her goal was to be the best writer she could and work for several magazines. She wanted a career as a staff writer on a panoply of topics and attack them with her clear, readable style and insight.

She wasn't able to read, or grade essays in the cramped office at the university with graduate students storming in and out. Instead, she brought everything home. She spent nights fabricating complex criticisms of undergraduate writing I'm not certain they could understand and appreciate.

We would have dinner as a family, visit a little at the dinner table, and Alice would have a drink and go to bed. I would read or do paperwork in the living room for about two hours, and I'd go to bed. Usually, nine o'clock at the latest.

Alice would usually be asleep. Early in the morning around two or three, she would go downstairs make herself another scotch and march up to the back bedroom to look at student essays or write. She was always ahead of her assignments and had begun work on a memoir. It focused on her difficult relationship with her mother, who had endured unhappiness for most of her marriage.

Their unhappiness was dumped upon her daughter who was powerless to do anything to change it. At this point, Alice wrote about fifteen thousand words of the memoir. Early each morning she would get out of bed and write, usually fueled by alcohol. As I woke and was ready for coffee and the day, she would return, getting whatever sleep she could before afternoon university classes.

She was barely forty and a strong young woman, so none of this showed. It was a pace, and her intellect and body could tolerate it. I didn't much like it, although felt it would all disappear once the degree was finished.

Alice never admitted to me that she was writing a memoir. Rather one afternoon I was snooping around the house and saw her manuscript that she had printed on a table in the back bedroom she used as her office. It was about half-complete, and I read a couple of the pages to get the feel of her writing and then warily left her office. For many authors, its bad luck to have someone read your book before it is complete.

Picking through the manuscript I came to the part of her story where her mother admitted to her that her father was impotent. That it was impossible to have intercourse. It was after Alice had turned eleven or twelve years old. To me that seemed to be putting an uncomfortable burden on an adolescent girl, who was just beginning to discover her own sexuality.

In a stream of consciousness, Alice had begun to tell the reader that this revelation made her see her father in a much different way. He was now vulnerable, weak, and therefore unable to protect her. This knowledge was the first and most profound disappointment that she had experienced from a man. It would follow her into the future.

SQUID

Thanksgiving was around the corner. Alice invited her parents to join the three of us and I looked forward to their company. After we bought all the food and planned the dishes, the preparation strangely seemed to have cloud of doom hanging over the day.

When they finally arrived, a sort of haze came over Alice's eyes. She sounded the same, looked the same, always smiling, yet there was something off that I could not quite account for. It was as if she were missing a beat or two in conversation.

I tried to convince myself it was my imagination playing tricks, though it wasn't. I had the feeling that Alice wanted to scream at them across the table yet restrained herself. Gone was the open and honest way she approached life. She was now careful and calculating, almost sinister, if I am being honest.

Her mother Jane had started talking about Chicago politics and the city mentality, which she did not like.

"The city doesn't have a mentality," Alice said across the table almost sharply.

"It does," her mother added.

"There are five million people here, and they don't think the same thing."

"Alice, you know what I mean," her mother said.

"I don't," Alice quickly interjected.

Automatically, I stood up, "I'd like some more turkey. Anyone else?"

"Bring me a wing," Sally chirped.

"Jane or Bob, anything?" I added.

They both smiled and shook their heads no. I went into the kitchen for the turkey. The rest of the dinner was pleasant, and the weather was mild. We all walked several blocks as a group admiring the Victorian architecture of the neighborhood. Back at the townhouse, there were a few minutes of innocuous conversation with Sally telling them about school.

Before long, her father rose, saying, "We must go. This has been a fabulous day. Thank you all." He marched to the closet after hugs for their fall coats.

Her mother announced at the door, "Christmas at our house, Ok?"

"Sounds good," I said.

Alice interrupted, "Let's see if we can figure out everyone's schedule. Life's pretty hectic."

Her father nodded, "You'll get a lot of time off from the university."

Alice noted, "It's hard to know, Dad. I am a teaching assistant, it pays the tuition, but they can give me work when everybody else is gone. I'll let you know."

When she closed the door and her parents started down the steps from our townhouse to the street, she turned to me. "I will find an excuse, any excuse. There's no way that I'm going to spend Christmas Day in that house."

I was only occasionally around her parents. They were rather convivial people much like my earlier set of in-laws. Sure, Joyce could get a bit dominating at times. Although I hit her limit during a few tenuous situations such as the custody arrangement I had initiated. In her mind, she figured I would simply disappear, and she assumed the raising of her granddaughter. She took it as her duty somehow. I had to remind her that things don't quite work that way, particularly with the law.

It was perhaps the worst, or at least the tensest, hour of my life at their trim Tudor house on Deloach Street. It was worse psychologically than anything I experienced in the military, and it was beyond my ability to change. That was Memphis.

If I had to guess, the problem was Alice's mother. Why would any woman tell her teenage daughter that her husband and the girl's father was impotent? That this aspect of their married life had ceased to exist. Did they bother with separate bedrooms? I don't think so. When I was last at their suburban house, I had used the upstairs bathroom on a visit because the downstairs one was occupied. Upstairs, there was Alice's old bedroom right next to it her brother Phil's. Thinking back, I assumed her mother might sleep in either one of the children's rooms if she wanted. But she

42

would have to go through the master to use her old bathroom. Alice was forty and they had been married two years before she was born. They had been a couple forty-two years. The average length of a marriage in the United States has fallen to seven years. After two children, did this thing repudiate her as a woman? Did it make her feel tarnished, unworthy and destroy her self-esteem? Why would she put that burden on a thirteen-year-old girl with no idea of what impotent meant?

I thought of my own family, which was sicker. My father was a brutal alcoholic and wife-beater. Perhaps my mother let herself get fat in some sort of defensive measure.

After Alice confessed about the impotency, I asked her what she thought of it now as a mature woman.

"I loved my parents, both. There was never any shouting or hatefulness. None."

I remember shrugging my shoulders, and saying, "I'm sure after ten or twenty years there are plenty of couples who face that sexless divide. And they stay together because they love everything else about each other."

She shook her head and informed me I missed what she had meant. She believed you should not tell your thirteen-year-old daughter that her father is impotent. "That was confusing and cruel and unnecessary."

"Can't you forgive her for bad judgement? Otherwise, she was a good and kind mother, made sure you did your homework, and watched out for drugs."

"Oh, the drugs, the Seventies. They found my brother in high school. He was kicked out for pushing a teacher down a small staircase and breaking her ankle. They sent him to a military school in Wisconsin, draining their life savings."

"The one in Florida?"

"Yes, him. There's nobody else."

"Impotency, or not, you were high school homecoming queen and went off to study architecture. I'd say you were levelheaded."

She nodded with nonchalance.

"My sister ended up in a mental hospital for eight months," I added.

"I know, I'm sorry," she said.

I agreed it was wrong for her mother to expect a thirteen-year-old girl to understand what male impotence meant and take that though life with her whenever she laid eyes on her father.

Alice walked around the living room in a tight circle. "My mother grew up in what should have been an ideal family. Her father was one of Denver's top surgeons in the 1930-40s. They had a huge house of eight bedrooms on a leafy street. But he died when she was a college student, and the family sort of fell apart."

Something clearly bothered her about her mother though. Maybe therapy might help but Alice was the sort of woman who would try that reluctantly and as a last resort, so I remained silent.

"You're a smart girl, you'll sort it out." I changed the topic back to the university and asked what she was writing. Her answer was conveniently vague. I figured that the memoir was swallowing all her time, every other night until three or four am.

Sally slept the righteous sleep of youth, and never heard Alice tiptoeing around or typing on the computer in the back bedroom.

We had a few friends over for dinner and in casual fashion, one wife asked what Alice was writing about, and she paused for a moment to think, "Oh, mostly long magazine articles. I started with architecture then went on to more general stuff, once I got into the swing of things."

"You'd like to write for magazines?" the wife continued in her inquiry.

"I'm not interested in newspapers," Alice answered with not much enthusiasm for the dinner conversation.

The friendly wife continued: "Oh, you'd be great at The Trib. Our neighbor in Evanston works there."

"Maybe I'll work for Cosmo someday, who knows?" Alice continued, wanting the conversation to be anything but about her.

Yet the woman plowed on, "You spent so much time in architecture, what made you leave?"

"You want the honest answer?" Alice asked.

"Yes."

"Boredom."

That brought an uncomfortable laugh from the husband.

"They passed me by on all the good commissions, and I got sick of it."

The conversation seemed a bit tense, and although Alice liked the woman, and tolerated her corporate husband, the night had come to a logical end.

The truth was that the owner denied Alice a head design commission. He inherited the architectural firm in 1964 (it had been founded in 1903). There were few women designing high rises in those days. The circle was not quite closed for women as architects, but it would take another six or eight years to break through. She simply got tired of waiting. Who could blame her?

I remember she had a shouting match with her boss over a design commission they had won for the state library. He told her he brought in a consultant who mostly taught at a local university though sometimes did design projects outside the school. Alice wanted to put that experience behind her.

She spent nearly half the time she devoted to her writing on the memoir. Consequently, she was always behind on her university assignments. They were less important to her since they were only about contemporary writing style away. She felt she had already mastered that.

The easiest subject for her to write on was Chicago history. That subject worked well for her because she was such a meticulous researcher, and nothing escaped her. She wrote stories on the beginning of the vast stockyards, on the turn of the century social reformers at Hull House, and the more colorful and crooked politicians who had almost disappeared from memory.

She wrote an article on the unique path of The Outfit, which was the local name for the Italian mafia. Her article included the unsolved murder of a mafia don on the golf course in Arlington Heights on an early autumn afternoon in 1971. The golf course was full, yet there were no witnesses to the killing. The man was found in the evening face down in one of the course's sand traps. It was a single shot in the back of the head from a small caliber pistol that many professional assassins favored. The police and the FBI treated it as a mob hit.

Life became a ritual. We would have dinner an hour after Alice got home. The two of us worked in the kitchen together. Unless we were hungry for a particular dish, it was something easy like pasta, steaks or hamburgers. We always had fruit on the table along with fresh-cut flowers. The flowers were something Alice insisted upon and picked them up a neighborhood florist a few blocks away.

Sally was doing well at the University of Chicago high school both academically and socially. And each evening was spent doing the copious homework assignments. She would eat with us, and we would talk a bit, then she would go upstairs. She listened to the radio most nights, and she was usually asleep by nine.

Miraculously she had made the switch from Memphis to Chicago well and seemed to thrive within the rigorous new school. She had a softened sort of teenage rebellion that was easy to deal with, or so it seemed.

One night, I made rib-eye steaks for us with a tossed salad. Alice was working in the living room correcting essays, which was part of her teaching assistant responsibility. She made this loud sound, and I stuck my head out of the kitchen.

She hollered, "Some of these kids can't write their way out of a paper bag. This stuff is frustrating. It's soulless."

"That can happen," I noted with a smile, and went back to the stove.

At dinner, we talked a little about the upcoming presidential election. When we asked Sally what she thought, she shrugged her shoulders, and said, "Nothing." The conversation going nowhere, Sally asked to be excused. She darted up the stairs to her bedroom and we heard her close the door.

I asked Alice if the master's program was still challenging.

"Not really. It's become routine once you know what kind of thing they want to see. You give 'em that. There is another semester of this nonsense, and the final project, which is supposed to be research. Yawn. How many Blacks report The Tribune editorials are racist? What percentage within a year? That kind of shit they call scholarship?"

I was doing well financially, and the household moved along smoothly. I only hoped everyone in it could be happy.

Joyce made noises she wanted Sally back there for Christmas, and I had said no. That it was disruptive. She accepted my decision with silence over the telephone. Not once since Sally arrived, had her mother called her. I assumed it was more of the same craziness and welcomed the silence.

That Saturday Alice headed off to her daylong seminar at the university and I beat a path to the Chicago Fish House. In their retail store, they were putting large whole squid on ice that looked perfect. I asked the older Italian counterman who worked there mornings if he cooked squid.

"These are primo, my friend," he said with a smile.

"How would you cook them?" I asked him.

"Like Napoli. You make squid in its own ink sauce."

He grabbed one of the squid off the ice and reached into its body cavity with his fingers. He felt around until he pulled out the dark black ink sack that the creature used to hide itself from predators and make an escape.

"You milk this sack with your fingers. Push it through the transparent wall, into a dish, and the black fluid will empty out."

I watched him closely through the glass case until I noticed black drops of liquid appear on his finger.

"You put this in a flying pan with cream and a little cornstarch, sauté it until it becomes thick. There is no smell like it. So strong you will think your standing in the bay of Naples. Cut the squid body into bite-size squares and fry them in butter and garlic. Get your pasta cooked and ready, dump it into a serving bowl, putting it aside. Cook the ink sauce and squid together, high heat, for maybe three minutes. Then dump it onto the pasta and mix. You'll never eat anything better."

He laughed as he handed me three large squid wrapped in butcher paper. With a wide smile on his face, he leaned over the counter: "I'll tell you this. After you've made this dish, your kitchen will smell like the ocean. Marvelous."

Once I was home and inside the kitchen, the progress of the squid dish appeared to go well. I squeezed the translucent ink sack through a metal strainer, and three sacks gave me about a quarter ounce of the black liquid. My fingers and the entire kitchen itself smelled like Davy Jones' locker. When the ink was mixed with the sautéed fresh squid, the whole first floor had a nautical aroma.

As I heard the front door open and recognized Alice's footsteps, she cried out. "What in God's name are you cooking? I can hardly breathe."

With the mixture cooking together on the gas, I yelled out, "Squid. In its own ink."

By this time, she was in the kitchen, shaking her head in dismay. "It'll take a week to air out the house. I'm not sure I want to eat this."

"It's a Neapolitan delicacy full of deep flavors," I stated.

"And you expect Sally to like this, right?"

As it happened, my ambition perhaps had reached its heights. Once on the table, only my plate had a heaping portion of the squid and pasta mixture. I dug into the liquorish-colored pasta with gusto. The flavor was so rich on my tongue that I began to sing the praises of my fishmongers who were now my associates, and close friends.

"This is easily the best pasta dish I've had in this town," I claimed between mouthfuls, "the flavors are deep and inquiring."

"It's kind of smelly," Sally added without being asked.

"That's the true smell of the sea, the real thing," I added with pride.

"I guess," Sally murmured.

Alice put her fork down and ran her hand through her dark long hair, and said, "I'll give you an A for originality. I would've never thought in a hundred years that you'd be sticking your fingers in the guts of a squid looking for an ink sack for dinner."

She reached across the table for the wine, and poured herself a second glass of wine, which was odd for her.

"To the maestro," she said holding her glass up and facing me. "You never cease to amaze me. You are a talented man, indeed." She drank half of it down in a single gulp.

Alice finished about a fourth of her pasta, Sally even less, but I took a second helping.

"Squid in its own ink will be my signature dish from now on," I proclaimed.

Alice shook her head and said none of our friends would ever eat it. They, or most everybody for that matter, were not that adventurous when it came to food.

"What?" I exclaimed. "It's Chicago, there are ten thousand restaurants, and you can get anything."

"Not the people we know. They do safe, what they know."

After dinner as usual Sally ran upstairs for the evening, and I told Alice that I would clean up. She concurred, mixed herself a neat scotch, and pulled a handful of papers out of her briefcase sitting comfortably on the couch.

"I need to find a thesis subject, which is a royal pain. They are already convinced I can write for magazines until the cows come home. I have no idea what to do, Jesus."

Finishing cleaning I saved what wine I had at dinner, and brought it to the living room, sitting down.

"Well, the money's alright with me, take your time, and do what you need to do."

"Thanks, that's good to know."

She sighed. "I'm tired. I'm going upstairs and read a few more of these essays until my eyes close." She bolted upright and left with the papers and her drink.

I had marketing plans to check myself; I sat there for a couple of hours, daydreaming and making occasional changes to the documents in front of me. After two hours, I decided to climb up the stairs to bed. I slowly made my way up. Alice was dead asleep with her reading light on and student essays across the bed. I cleaned up the papers putting them on her nightstand and turned out the light.

I woke up around four to the siren of a police cruiser a couple of streets away and I reached over to touch Alice, though she was gone. Sitting up in bed, I could see a light at the end of the hallway and heard the keys of her computer click in a fast cadence. She was at the memoir again. It had become an obsession. My instinct was to tell her to come back to bed, though I let that go and turned over and went back to sleep for another hour before the alarm.

When the alarm went off, she was back in bed and slept through it. I got up, showered, dressed. Then I made a light breakfast for everyone before Sally ran out the door to catch her ride to school on the Southside.

Before I left for the office, I walked to her back bedroom office and clicked her desktop computer keyboard. When the screen illuminated, I typed in her password which I knew and saw her book file in front of me on the screen. With another click I had the manuscript open in front of me.

There was more about her father this time. However, most of it was about the resentment she felt having to take on the misery of her mother and the barren marriage. Page after page discussed how she wanted to scream with rage at having to shoulder that knowledge.

After the confession, her parents never made any effort to resolve the issue. They never sought counseling, or at worse they didn't separate and attempt to start a life with someone else. It was hidden and perhaps accepted at some level. Her mother obviously resented it but to the outside world, nothing seemed different. Her brother continued to invite trouble into his own life and maybe this secret was part of the reason.

The memoir had now become Alice's obsession. Her nighttime drinking and writing didn't seem healthy. On the contrary, she dropped her gym membership and appeared tired and drawn. Yet she continued to drink scotch.

Youth seemed to protect her. She was always there for Sally to talk to if she wanted or needed. And the two of them might make an Italian dish one night a week. However, it seemed like that only happened every few weeks at that point.

As the Christmas season approached, we decorated the house with garlands on the mantle and red candles in the large front windows. Then it was time to pick a tree, and we made an event out of it, visiting two or three lots. We tied our seven-foot tree on top of the car after we stopped for hot chocolate at an Austrian bakery. We bought a Stollen cake too for the holiday. It was my weakness, the Stollen.

Alice got Sally some stylish clothes and I added a few silly gifts. We had promised to give each other one inexpensive gift.

As we got closer to Christmas, Alice decided she wanted a holiday party. We quickly surveyed a handful of friends and found an evening they'd all be free. Feverishly, we began to get ready. We would have liquor, wine and a holiday eggnog punch spiked with Jamaican rum. Sally had gotten her grandmother Joyce's recipe for her crab and cheddar dip, and that would be her culinary contribution.

One late afternoon I had gotten home from the office and Alice was sitting in the dark in the living room with a drink. She was looking off into space even as she must have heard me open and close the front door.

Walking over to her, she seemed listless, and I asked, "Are you alright?" To which she simply nodded.

"You know," she said. "I was thinking that my parents should've been divorced. They stopped loving each other a long time ago. But they never had the courage. I think my father was afraid to leave, and I don't know why."

"Why beat yourself up over this? God, most marriages are on life support. That is the bane of modern life. Your parent's generation, stayed together because everyone else did, miserable or not."

Alice looked up at me and smiled, "You're probably right."

She got up and took her empty glass to the kitchen and put it on the counter before returning.

"Lately she's gotten involved in politics, volunteering for Jesse Jackson. She has never known a Black person either as a child in Denver, or here as a married woman. My father tells me on the telephone that she's going off her rocker."

I laughed. "Well, he's a conservative Republican I'm imagining, and her behavior startles him out of his stupor."

"They're late middle age, maybe a lot unhappy, I don't know. But they depend on each other. You tell me they don't have many friends, it's just them."

"Pretty much," she said without emotion.

"You can't fix their lives, stop trying," I told her.

"I haven't lifted a finger," she said.

"Alright, what I meant is stop thinking about them, and their problems. It's starting to creep into your own life."

"They've always been in my life."

"But it's starting to take its toll. And you're drinking too much to chase it away."

"What the hell are you talking about?" She said.

"I mean you're drinking into the early morning, and that's crazy. Aren't you worried about this, or is there something about us you don't like?"

It was time for me to stop, and I knew it. I had hit a nerve when I mentioned overdoing the alcohol, and her mouth was set in anger.

"I just want us to be happy," I said with contrition.

Just then, the door opened, and Sally entered. Looking at both our drawn faces, she said, "Something wrong? Should I go upstairs?"

"No," said Alice, "I have a real Italian dinner planned and I need some help. You game?"

"You bet," Sally said. "I'll do anything to escape those sea monsters."

When it was time to trim the tree, I made a mulled wine for us, and we each put ornaments on the tree. Alice disappeared upstairs and returned with a small blue box. She laid it on the carpet on the side of the tree. Opening it, I could see that it was filled with little metal cans that had been perforated to accommodate a wire handle. Inside each can had a small bouquet of plastic flowers.

"What are these?" I asked her, looking closely at a can that had been painted gold.

"My mother was diagnosed with tuberculosis when I was two years old. In those days, they sent you away to a sanitarium for a time, to cure. She was there for a year. These are the Gerber baby food cans from that year. My father felt he couldn't take care of me properly by himself. So, my mother's brother and his young wife who were childless took me for that year. They lived in Denver."

For some reason her aunt and uncle saved a few of these cans and gave them to her father. It was a strange gift, and he made Christmas ornaments from them.

It was difficult to know exactly where the problems Alice had with her parents came from. I thought the source of the problems could be any of these things or, it could be something else completely.

Our Christmas Party was a success. Sally carried trays of appetizers to the hungry crowd while Alice and I maintained the strenuous kitchen duty. We became a tag-team of host and hostess. I poached a whole Atlantic salmon who with its regal head guarded the dinner buffet. It became the centerpiece. We made three different kinds of dips to go with it including the classic dill.

Alice who had a shy side stood in front of the Christmas tree with Sally and she led everyone singing Deck the Halls and Silent Night. My heart almost burst with the pride I felt at that spectacle. It was one of those exquisite moments, and my eyes teared up as they finished Silent Night. Then everyone in the living room gave out a loud Christmas cheer and went for what was left of the eggnog and desserts.

As we cleaned up after Sally went to bed, I told Alice this was easily the best night of my life. I had never felt happier or had loved anything more than those few hours of our Christmas party. I hugged her, and gently kissed her parted lips, saying, "You've made me the happiest of men. With everything you do. Taking care of Sally, there's no one like you."

"You're going to make me cry if you keep this up.," she whispered wiping her own eyes that had begun to tear.

Looking back, I don't know quite what it was that troubled Alice. Yet it was something deeply seeded and far beyond my powers to fix. I seemed powerless to stop this train careening down the track to destroy her.

After we had cleaned up, Alice said she wanted to sit in the living room with her thoughts before going to bed. She promised she would not be long. But she stayed downstairs maybe another two hours, having another drink starring out the window onto the dark tree-lined street, her thoughts somewhere unknown to me. I recall coming down the steps and seeing her standing in front of the window with her head on the ice-cold pane. It seemed an uncomfortable thing to do.

"Come on to bed," I murmured softly. "You need a good night's rest after throwing such a fabulous party."

"It was, wasn't it?" she asked, almost cooing.

"The finest."

"And Sally was such a big girl, the perfect hostess," she added.

"Because she learned from the best," I stated. "Now, it's bedtime."

"Alright," she said, turning and following me up the stairs, singing softly, "Old King Wenceslaus on the feast of Stephen," and then suddenly broke it off.

Her parents came Christmas Day for an early dinner. We made a goose, stuffed with a wonderful mixture of hazelnuts and pate. I made the pate the day before. I took a pound of fresh chicken livers I got from our neighborhood German butcher, chopped them finely in our blender. Then I added a half pound of ground fresh pork sausage, Herbes de Provence, three ounces of chopped hazelnuts in a bath of hazelnut oil, ten garlic cloves, fresh sorrel, dry milk powder, nutmeg and Kosher salt and one egg. Once mixed it had the consistency of mud and I stored it covered in the fridge until we would fill the goose.

The stuffing was my idea. I followed a recipe from the French-born chef at the nearby Bakery restaurant. He was going to make it for his own family on New Year's Day. It consisted of a light pate but the number of garlic cloves inside the pate made it far too pungent for most American palates. At the table, Alice's father let out this loud burp from it much to his embarrassment. Naturally we all laughed, teasing him about his usual bland diet for the past decade. In his defense however, he suffered from stomach acid issues for many years. I had chosen a Riesling from Alsace, and we drank it chilled with the roast goose. It made the perfect companion for a Christmas dinner. Admittedly, the goose may have been a bit greasy, but the Riesling helped with digestion. In fact, it took two bottles to find our way through the main course.

The Christmas season was wonderful, highlighted by snow on Christmas Eve, which made it the more special.

MUSSELS

Right before New Year's Day, I got a call from Sally's grandparents Joyce and Tucker to tell me that they were coming to Chicago for a day and a night. She asked if Sally might stay with them at the hotel while they were here. I readily agreed because I knew it was something Sally would want because she adored Joyce.

True to form, she showed up on the doorstep, dressed in her signature pastel St. John's outfit with matching skirt and jacket and black high heels. Inside she offered a small gift to Alice for our hospitality before sitting down to chat for a moment before she left.

"This is such a lovely house, so historic. But these being so close makes me a bit claustrophobic," she said.

"It's a big city. The whole block was built in 1895 for railroad managers, all the houses are the same red brick design."

"That's marvelous," she noted. "Sally has adapted well, it seems."

"She has, it's her home," I said.

"It's been such a short time for her. I think she considers Memphis home."

I could see that Alice was losing her patience dealing with Joyce's condescension, and I felt the same.

Quickly, I said, "You and Sally are eager to start your big adventure. Let me call you a taxi, it'll only take five minutes."

"Thank you," she said, "It was so nice to see you, Alice."

"And you too, Joyce," Alice said moving from the living room toward the door.

In less than five minutes, a taxi was at the door, and we were free of the woman. Alice made herself a whiskey and asked if I wanted one, and I nodded yeah.

"I think that's the phoniest person I've ever met, such disgusting pretension," Alice noted as she made the drinks.

"She does that to overcome low self-esteem, puts herself on this artificial pedestal. After all these years doing it, she's come to believe it herself."

Alice sat on the couch next to me shaking her head. "I hope I never have to suffer her company again."

"I promise you won't."

Alice changed the subject to a cross-country skiing trip in Wisconsin the three of us had been invited to join. We talked about what fun we could have at this remote lodge.

What hurt me most about dealing with Joyce and Tucker through this custody controversy was they had this sort of condescending attitude. It was surely based on my humble coal-town background, and they were therefore superior. It was in the way they positioned themselves in a parental role, easily forgetting I was the child's father. For them, it was a matter of them being in her life first, and more solvent.

It was true that they had gifted Nancy and me that small Memphis home. They provided a few things that made Sally's life seemingly better like summer trips to their lake house and lavish Christmas gifts. That was it, little more.

Had I gone to court, it would have been messy. I had hard evidence of their daughter's indifference and neglect of Sally. Her sister's concern would aid my case, but truth does not always win out in domestic dramas. Unsavory actions and events often tend to be forgotten or never happened for some.

Dealing with Joyce could only be termed as annoying. It was easy to tolerate, the rest of the outside world was far more problematic and scarier. The divorce had come quickly, and custody was shared, negotiated between the parents. It was a simple finale as these things go. Then her sister intervened, and the playing field changed. It was leveled.

The last day of Joyce's visit, she dropped Sally off with two or three large shopping bags of new school clothes purchased at Saks. There was a kiss and a hug on the front porch, and she was gone. To Sally it was an exciting visit with her much-adored grandparents. As soon they were gone, she quickly got back to her life in Chicago, calling several school friends that very night.

The harsh Midwest winter came and went. We managed to spend a weekend in February in Wisconsin at the Wolf River Lodge cross-country skiing. Sally took to the sport right away. Before long, spring made itself known again with the budding trees on the block.

In early May, Tucker suffered a massive stroke at his office downtown. The prognosis for his recovery was slim. His heart was seriously damaged, and with no prospect for rehabilitation, he was sent home. I took Sally down to Memphis myself so she could spent time with her grandfather and say goodbye.

Tucker and Joyce were always decent to me. They were even friendly in so many ways, particularly on the summer weekends at their lake in Saulsbury. In those years, I would fish with Tucker many evenings and we would usually catch enough bass or brim to feed the family. Sally swam in the lake as a naked toddler. I saved the pictures to show guests when she weds.

Mercifully, Tucker didn't linger too long. He could speak and recognized those around him until the very end. He passed away in his sleep a month after he left the hospital. Sally would attend the funeral, and I asked Joyce if I might attend with her.

She replied, "I'd rather you didn't come to be honest. She can spend that time with her mother."

I put Sally on the plane for a two-day stay in Memphis. She did in fact accompany her mother to the funeral home and the church for a memorial and finally at the gravesite. Tucker was a popular man locally and fifty or sixty people said their farewell at his grave. In a condolence note later, I told Joyce I had always liked her and Tucker, and I felt bad that circumstance had made us adversaries.

Sally told me her mother had almost nothing to say throughout the whole thing. They barely talked about anything else either. Nancy's sister and her husband stood next to them, and she gave them half a hug, which was the extent of their contact. The intervention concerning custody caused this irretrievable chasm.

Back in Chicago, Sally went about the business of being a student again albeit sad at the passing of her grandfather. She really had a closer bond with Joyce. Joyce had wanted Sally to become her third daughter, or a replacement for her first daughter so it seemed. It was difficult to know which.

After Tucker's death, Joyce became needier of Sally's company. When we mentioned that we might all go to France for the month of June with one of Alice's friends who had a large farmhouse in Burgundy, Joyce became undone.

"That's my time with Sally, you can't do that," she said on the telephone almost spitting the words.

I told her calmly, "We agreed that we'd work together. It is something I don't have to do but I promised Sally that she would have time with both sides of the family. Just be reasonable. This time in France will be a marvelous adventure for her."

"I want her here, the day after you come back, do you understand?" she announced angrily.

I did not go for the bait. Avoiding confrontation, I calmly said, "I'm sure we can balance Sally's schedule, so she sees all the people she loves. We'll work it out, don't worry."

The trip to France didn't happen because our friend who was an interior designer got a law school commission and that cancelled Europe for her. However, her family had a Wisconsin lake home at Delavan her father bought twenty years ago, and rarely visited. That getaway became the backbone of our spring and early summer antics when Sally was in Chicago.

Alice's progress at the university, the class portion at least, went well and she received A's. Now only the shadow of the thesis stood in the way of the degree. Finding a research topic was always tricky. Oddly, she took her fascination with words from the countless crossword puzzles she did weekly.

She decided to monitor the growth of key words, and terms in the change of attitudes and behaviors. She chose the term 'acid rain' and measured its relative frequency in American and Canadian daily newspapers over a 6-month period, to gauge its acceptability as a standard of popular scientific definition in English-language. With computer searches, she would track how often it appeared in articles and determine its potential for becoming a permanent language icon.

Alice knew computers from architecture, and now the university mainframe would facilitate her search. At the end of each of the six months, she collected her data from the mainframe, and then employed the computer to analyze the results.

It was more technical than I cared to know about. Yet she was on top of it, and on the last day had a complete analytical breakdown and would start her thesis. She would need 50 pages with a five-page introduction and one page conclusion. She set to it and within a month of working until morning with a couple of whiskeys by her side, the thesis was complete. She had a professional proofreader to format it and was ready to present it a month before it was due.

Her Saturday seminars continued, and I made my usual trek to the Chicago Fish House and Sam's for the right wine accompaniment. One day I noticed they had a fine haul of fresh mussels. Mussels was not something I generally noticed, so I bought a couple dozen. If any shellfish smells like the bottom of the ocean, it is the humble mussel. It stinks of a muddy bottom.

Once in the kitchen they required scrubbing that took a half an hour to clean them. I sautéed a few cloves of garlic in butter and added most of a bottle of a fine Napa chardonnay from the Franciscan vineyard that was very buttery in taste. I put the mussels in the steamer and cranked up the heat. It was an aroma, like nectar from King Neptune.

Before I started the process, I had bought some large Idaho potatoes and julienned them into thin strips. I cooked them once in hot olive oil, dried them, and let them sit for a few minutes. Then cooked them a second time to insure their crispness.

Before long, Sally had come down for dinner and Alice was hovering trying to relax from a busy seminar. I asked Alice to cut the two large baguettes I'd gotten. We would need them to soak up the succulent mussel juices.

When the food was on the table, we all dug into the black half open shells with our small forks extricating the fat creatures. We enjoyed them with a mouthful of pomme frites, dipping the crusty bread in its juices as we went along. All this was paired with cool Chardonnay that was on the table. It was a feast for a king, and a little butter on the chin was not a problem for these three diners.

With a huge bowl of empty shells in front of her, Alice commented triumphantly, "That was one of the best meals - no, correction - that was the best meal I've ever had."

We laughed, and Sally said, "I thought I didn't like mussels, until now."

Sally soon tiring of adult conversation went up to her room to talk with school friends as she did most nights before bed.

Alice comfortable on the couch leaned on me and gave me a rundown on what she needed to do to finish the degree.

"Dickerson said it's good, and if he likes it the other two on the committee will, so I'm home free. With some effort, I can finish the other thing that has been lingering. Write the damn thing."

"What's that?" I asked, knowing the answer. The book she needed to write.

"Just some book idea I'm trying to get done. It's taking forever."

"What's the subject?" I asked, curious as to what she would tell me.

"Not good luck to talk about something that's not finished. Might jinx it." She turned toward me with a serious look on her face, "Really, I don't want to talk about it, alright?"

"Sure. Tell me about it when you're done," I said.

Alice leaned over and kissed me on the cheek, "I'm so grateful for you allowing me to do this, paying for it all. It has meant the world to me. When I get the degree, I can't wait to get back to work, whatever writing job it is."

"If you're happy, I'm happy," I said and meant every word. "I'll never forget how you picked up with Sally as if you'd been with her from the beginning."

She told me that Sally was one of the easiest teenagers she had ever been around, never sullen or obstinate, and full of life.

The madness of Alice's nighttime memoir scribbling and drinking continued. It was a prolonged secret agony or obsession. I could never quite determine which. Her thesis was already researched, written and presented to the university with the same focus and professionalism she brought to her years in architecture. This was something else, something entirely different and more sinister that I couldn't quite fathom. I could see what was happening as the scotch bottle quickly went down each day replaced by another by the end of the week.

She was nonchalant about things in her back office, though her desk was always neat and orderly, piles of paper perfectly squared. If Alice went out for a long errand during the week, or was off to the daylong seminar on Saturday I could look at what she had written.

That Saturday as she left early, and Sally had stayed the weekend in Hyde Park with girlfriends, I went to the back bedroom to look at her memoir.

Her book file was right there on the desktop screen, and I clicked on it to get a look. She had already written almost forty thousand words on the subject. It was mostly a stream of consciousness about how she felt about herself, and her immediate family, all rather bittersweet.

The one thing that seemed missing was anything about me. There were maybe ten pages on her post-college boyfriend from Connecticut. She wrote about how she'd gotten pregnant, and after much thought she'd decided to get an abortion. One of her girlfriends whom I had met accompanied her to the clinic that performed it. Then her friend drove her home to the small apartment in Lincoln Park. She had taken two days off from work to recover. There was a bad flu going around the city that winter, and literally, everybody took time off from work. In three days, she was back at her drawing table drafting floor plans for some high-rise.

There was maybe five pages on her younger brother and all his trouble in school. She wrote about him being kicked out for drug use and unsavory behavior, and finally all the family consternation led them to send him to an obscure military school. He managed almost two years there though failed to graduate. Afterward he moved to south Florida with his high school girlfriend who was working downtown.

Alice described some of the shouting matches between her brother and parents. She wrote about the painful and expensive decision to send him away to boarding school. At the time, he had quit high school. He was sleeping until noon and going out at night with his friends until the early morning.

The most violent incident was when he pushed his father down the three short steps at the side of the house, where he fell into the flowerbed. Seeing what he had done, her brother helped his father up from the ground, hugging him. At heart, he was a decent kid though terribly confused. They chose the military academy from a family friend's recommendation. They looked at the school brochures together around the kitchen table. Without argument, everyone agreed it was the best next step for the family.

All that I read seemed rather normal for any middle class suburban American family in 1970 with similar issues. However, it didn't really explain what was happening to Alice, this seemingly destructive path.

I logged out of the computer and started down the stairs where I would spread a few client-marketing plans on the coffee table. I'd clean them up before tomorrow's presentation.

ROYAL REDS

Being Saturday morning, I needed to make a pilgrimage to the Chicago Fish House first to see what surprise they had for dinner. I hurried there and noticed a pile of fresh shrimp in the glass case that was a bit redder in color than the usual Gulf types and asked about them.

They were Royal Reds, just in season. They derived their crimson color from a nutrient-dense diet. Supposedly, the flesh was lighter and sweeter than the typical shrimp, closer to lobster. I was convinced and I bought two pounds for an Italian dish I had wanted to make, Shrimp Scampi.

Italian immigrants brought the dish to America in the 1890s. They couldn't find the larger crustacean, langostino they had known and loved in the old country, so they used Royal Reds instead. They called it Scampi and substituted locally harvested shrimp.

Excited to try making the dish, I called an Italian friend who was a chef and asked him if he had ever made Scampi. He laughed, "How can you grow up in an Italian family and not make Scampi? Please."

His recipe was to melt a half pound of butter in a skillet, add a fourth of a cup of Italian parsley (which I wisely bought), lemon juice, three large cloves of garlic, basil, a tablespoon of Worcestershire sauce, half a teaspoon of Tabasco, and salt and, of course, white wine. You sauté until everything is translucent and put it to the side.

I arranged the Royal Reds with their tails like the British redcoat army inside a baking pan and poured over the liquid mixture. Baking time was fifteen minutes maximum, just enough to turn the red creatures nearer to pink.

I served the Scampi with a dry Sauvignon Blanc, and lots of fresh Italian bread, and the ladies dived into it without a second thought. Jokingly, with her mouth full, Alice remarked, "You've earned your culinary laurels, you've learned to cook like an Italian."

"More, more," Sally begged, holding her plate out to be filled with Royal Reds.

I had to admit that with all the butter and garlic, this had to be one of the most succulent meals I'd ever eaten. It was easy to understand why this dish was on literally every Italian restaurant menu in this country, and in Europe.

There were some weeks where Alice might let a couple of days go by without returning to the manuscript in middle of the night. Although, it was hard to predict when she would work on the memoir. Some nights we would sit in the living room, reading or talking and the hours before bedtime passed uneventfully. Other nights she would return to her writing and the ritual continued.

As time went on, I became cautious about sneaking into her office to read what she had written. I hoped there was something in it that would give me a clue to what was wrong. I hoped to find out how to help her overcome it. She had written fifty thousand words, and there were only perhaps two paragraphs about me, and I was not named. It made me think that I was blameless in the breakdown she must be experiencing.

Our physical life had come to a standstill. There might be interest from her in lovemaking once in two weeks. I thought she may have ceased to find me attractive any longer, but it was hard to fathom. I wondered if it could be the added responsibility for Sally. Certainly, her contribution was a lot to ask, and it had taken its toll. However, when I watched her around Sally it seemed that this was her happiest times. She was animated and always smiling. They could talk about anything together and often did. Sally never came to me telling tales or expressing displeasure with Alice.

It seemed she bore the entire burden of her mother's unhappiness in the marriage. It seemed like this responsibility, which she continued to shoulder was too much.

When we were alone for a weekend with Sally in Hyde Park, I asked her directly what was bothering her. Was it me? What had I done, or not done? Was the Sally thing too much to ask of her? I also stated that the burden of getting a master's was more than enough to be derailed.

She was thoughtful in response. "I'd say that I don't know what you're talking about, though I do. For some reason I can't tell you what's exactly wrong."

I thought it was time to really look at myself. Why wasn't this seemingly placid life working out? What was the disconnect? Had we hurried too quickly to become committed? Did I thrust Sally upon her without giving her a chance to find out if she wanted to live with me as a couple, as husband and wife?

All I wanted was to come home to a household at peace, feel some degree of love for one another, and be comfortable in our own skins. I wanted to get as much as I possibly could: money, house, car, wife and children.

My daughter attended one of the best schools in the country. My wife was an architect and a journalist; I was a writer and businessman. We had friends; we went to the symphony and the theatre and art openings. We were on the right path to whatever dream I had inside my head. I was far away from the coal town where I grew up, away from the abuse and misery of my own family. Maybe I wasn't authentic enough with Alice, hadn't gone deep enough inside me.

Instead, I had given her a fabricated image of what I thought she might want from that supposed right man in her life. Maybe it was all false. I didn't know the truth, mostly because I had always been afraid. It was easier to invent my own version. I began to blame myself for what seemed to be happening to Alice. I believed I was the actual cause of the unwinding of her sanity. It was not her mother, her father, or her rebellious brother. It was me. I was responsible for this tragedy.

Maybe I started hot with Alice. Perhaps I put her in the spotlight right away and once she was comfortable, I created the blueprint for a lifelong relationship. Then, I would pull out the rug. I would slowly start removing those things I didn't like, with the intention of changing her to fit my own expectation of who she was. I would nudge her from the bosom of her success in architecture to the rocky shoals of writing which meant constant dissonance. I had repeatedly encouraged her to take the plunge.

I knew advertising writers at big agencies and columnists at the Chicago Tribune who were hacks. In their hearts, they knew they were miserable. Someone along the way who was no longer important said they had had talent. But only enough talent to hit a ceiling after a couple of years. I should have stayed out of Alice's way in that sense, stop acting as puppet master, subtly pulling the strings.

It was only to make me feel better. To remake her in my eyes of what she should be, and once she became that, then maybe I would be satisfied. It wasn't her ambition, it was my own, couched in the subtle nudge to have her do something that allowed me to say I had made it, whether behind the scenes or not. That was a confusing way to assuage my own battered ego. My earlier marriage to Sally's mother made me an object because I was not ready. I was forced to react to her needs and that of her parents, who were the ultimate puppet masters. It murdered whatever independence I possessed, and I saw no way to escape. So, I pushed back behind the scenes, made every day either argumentative, or an unhappy capitulation. Her will, and if you add an infant to the mix, would always triumph.

I hated every minute of it. I hated being handed a script on how to behave with these people. I stuffed it away for as long as I could before I would simply explode. Now, with Alice I would be in charge, I would take on the role of puppet master at last. I saw what I did as benign, though was it? Hardly, if I were to be truthful.

The university graduate committee with many compliments accepted her thesis. She was asked by the department head to present it at a communications conclave in San Diego as a featured speaker. She practiced her presentation aloud for a week, and on the designated dates, she flew to the West Coast accompanied by the university department director who would introduce her work at the conference.

Always practiced in her methods, her presentation was received well. Later as the audience milled around waiting for the next speaker, a stocky bald man with a winning smile approached her.

"May I be the first to congratulate you on your work, first rate," he said. "I'm Willard Brownlee. Director of Stanford's new media initiative, launched last month by a sixty million grant from Apple. We are anxious to find outstanding scholars to anchor our doctorate program, and I'd like you to join us. The application would be a mere formality after what I heard you say this morning." Still smiling, he handed Alice his business card.

"Why thank you, Doctor Brownlee," was all that Alice could manage to say at the moment.

"It's fully funded, there's no expense to you. And you'd be part of the Stanford junior faculty which is an honor."

"Goodness," Alice said, "It certainly is. How long would the program study last?"

"Two years, possibly three."

Again, he smiled. "I'll admit too, that we will have the finest hardware in the entire world on campus. Everything is in place for you to succeed."

"That sounds fantastic," Alice added with a slight blush because of his attention.

"Please give the opportunity some thought," Brownlee added in parting and shook her hand goodbye.

As he stepped away, he turned to her, "Call me in a week, I'll be waiting," and with a wave he left her.

The significant part was that Alice was dead drunk at that moment. She told me years later that everything about that day was a faint blur.

On the plane back to Chicago, she told her professor about the encounter and showed him the business card. He shook his head knowingly: "You've got no choice. A chance like this happens once in a lifetime. Stanford has the best computer scientists in the world, who would be ready to push your research way ahead. Nobody I know had a chance like that."

Although Alice felt elated by the recognition, California was as remote to her as Bolivia. The trip to San Diego was her first time in the state. Frankly, all it had been was a shuttle ride from the airport to the Sheraton hotel at Coronado. It was sunny of course and she noticed bathers outside her hotel room window. That was pretty much it. A conference dinner was held in a large meeting room for two hundred participants with several speakers. It was rubber chicken and not very exciting.

When she told me about the encounter, I marveled at the possibilities. "We could live in San Francisco, and you'd drive down to Palo Alto. The business is portable, I see six or seven corporate clients twice a year, and they don't care where I live."

"God," she said, "it's tempting. I would get away from my parents and their troubles. Clear my head."

"He said a scholarship, full ride," I reiterated.

"Yeah, maybe there would be undergraduate teaching or research assistance, I don't know."

"We could go out and look it over for weekend; Sally could go to Memphis, which she'd love. You could see if you really want it. Be a big change."

That's what we did; we made it a pleasure trip. We stayed at a boutique hotel off Union Square with a gourmet Italian restaurant in the lobby and rented a car for a trip to Stanford the next day.

We left after rush hour, and it still was fifty minutes to traverse what appeared to be seventeen miles of interstate. Traffic was horrendous.

Inside Palo Alto, it was easy to find Stanford. I parked at a visitor's lot, while she found the right building, which was five minutes away. In the meantime, I amused myself at the student union center. I found a gourmet café inside with magazines and newspapers, though it seemed that everyone else in the room was on some sort of electronic device. Welcome to Silicon Valley, I mused.

Alice was absent for two hours and found me reading at the café.

"Well, how did it go?" I asked her with excitement.

She dropped into the leather chair next to me and let out a big sigh. "Very focused and intense people. But with a façade of casualness. It was with Doctor Brownlee and two computer scientists. They read my research paper and told me that they were interested in language patterns, behavior, and its predictability. This is not journalism. It is something entirely different. It's an attempt at a futuristic look of language, quite complicated."

Alice sighed again, and asked me to get her a coffee, which I did, and she sipped it several times before speaking.

"The good news was they see me fitting into Stanford's push for new media, language, and models for analyzing human relationships with the written word. This isn't magazine writing or being a novelist. It's being a scientist, and I'm not sure I want that."

I shook my head, "Then say no, walk away, and we'll go back to Chicago. Maybe you'll work for the Tribune, or AP, once you graduate."

"That's my feeling, honestly. This is worth two hundred thousand dollars, and I could probably teach at Cal Tech after if I wanted. But I don't want to; I just want to write, period."

I stood up, "Fine, let's say goodbye to Stanford, and have dinner on Fisherman's Wharf with the tourists tonight."

"Sounds good," Alice said and threaded her arm through mine as we walked toward the rental car.

Back in Chicago, Alice found a date to defend her thesis. That afternoon late, she came home with a broad smile on her face. "Defense flawless, degree gotten. Hooray."

Since it was a weeknight, we grabbed Sally and made a beeline for her favorite Mexican restaurant under the El tracks with the city's best beef tacos to celebrate.

Now that she achieved her master's degree, Alice went back to her memoir, which I don't think she ever left. I had not paid much attention to it for a while, and with this Saturday her final university seminar, I did take another peek. She was about finished I thought. She had written nearly eighty thousand words, and it was clearly a book-length manuscript. Usually memoirs are shorter, most novella length.

Near the end, I found pages where she talked about our relationship. It was more critical than I had hoped. She discussed her concern about my subtle manipulation. She touched on how I used outspokenness to trick her into changing who she was only to please me.

She claimed that I wanted to rule her life and make her into a Stepford wife. She used the term from the 1970s movie, and believed it was part of my plan of dominance. Increasingly, she could not be herself around me. I wanted her skinnier, younger, and some idea of superwoman that I had conjured up, probably because my own mother was such a mess. I was never direct with her or loving. Those attempts at sex were only for me. I acted as if I cared about her pleasure when I clearly did not.

It took me aback to read the words and gave me pause to think. Had I done any of this she talked about on purpose, or had she really misunderstood me? None of us is perfect; she no doubt faked orgasms before. Sure, that would be for my benefit, but it also allowed her to end the lovemaking, calling it finished.

She said I was getting paunchy and that was a turn-off. I touched my stomach, and thought, I'd better add the gym to my weekly routine. I had put on ten extra pounds in a year. What I read were small digs, except for the accusation of manipulation. That accusation undid me because I felt innocent of the charge. I only worked to make things better as a couple, and did not see myself as an egomaniac, or crude. I had known men who easily fit that category and never felt it something I wanted to emulate.

I imagined what Alice wrote was what she believed to be true. However, what was absent from the writing was how to change it. Was her answer to drink more and see that self-medication as the solution to her mother's terminal unhappiness or her father's dismal of his conjugal rights?

CRAB CAKES AND RISOTTO

I was determined to talk to Alice about her drinking. I would offer to cut back with mine, or completely stop if it would help her. The fact was that she had three or four strong whiskeys every night. That obviously cannot be healthy. The effect showed in her night owl hours, the dark circles under her eyes, and the change in personality. She had become hypersensitive to most everything. It was easy to offend her with a word, or a gesture.

Saturday rolled around. I pointed my mustang in the direction of the Chicago Fish House. By now, the staff knew me by name. As I walked in the door, one of the clerks called out to me. He told me they had gotten a planeload of fresh Dungeness crab from the West Coast. I had been unsuccessful in my decade's long search for the perfect crab cake, so I bought half-dozen crabs to clean myself for the meat. It was a lot of work but ensured that the crabmeat was fresh. With hammer, screwdriver and metal claws, I struggled for at least an hour removing the flesh. I ended up with a nice pile of crabmeat for four very substantial patties and I set to work.

I had bought fresh chives which I sliced into small pieces and mixed them into the crab along with my own French breadcrumbs I made earlier during the week. I only added just enough to give it texture. Next, I took the bottle of Duke's mayonnaise out of the refrigerator. The secret is to make your own or use Duke's as there are no other options. I added half the jar and threw in two eggs for four thick patties. For a subtle but distinct hotness, I used a quarter teaspoon of cayenne peppers I dried and crushed.

I made four thick flat patties out of the crab and coated the outside with a mixture of Panko and crumbs made from the stale baguette. I brushed them with an egg wash on both sides and put them into a cast iron frying pan with a load of butter on intense heat. The cooking time is by eye and smell, and only turn the patties over once to ensure brownness on both sides.

Look, I have eaten crab cakes in Boston, Charleston and low country small towns, Savannah and New Orleans. I'll admit that most of them were inedible. They were either undercooked or overcooked, the breadcrumbs often resembled cardboard, or apple crumble. I have paid anywhere from seven dollars to seventy for the premier crab cake and have been universally disappointed, and yes, in the finest restaurants. Chefs do not know how to do it right; the perfect crab cake is perhaps a myth.

Pleased with myself, I served them to the girls with an arugula and French breakfast radish salad with a mustard vinaigrette. We drank a Pino Grigio.

"What do you think?" I asked Alice after she took her first bite, and she smiled. "You've done it."

It was my turn to try the crab cake. Slowly I used the side of the fork to break through the hardened breadcrumb exterior until I was able to get a moist forkful of the crab. I put in my mouth and chewed slowly with my eyes closed.

"Ah, I'm close," I said, "though not quite there yet."

They both started to laugh, and said in unison, "You're wrong."

What should have been the best years of life had an undercurrent that was not going away. If Alice drank a bit as a college student and a young adult, out with friends, what happened now was a freefall. Nobody drinks three or four strong whiskeys in a night's time and not have a problem. It became evident to me, and no doubt, it was easily recognizable to her. Or was it? I heard her slur her words in conversation with me. I had never heard that before, ever. She accepted it as normal.

Certainly, nothing like this could have been normal to her. If she were still at the architectural firm, maybe her hand would start to shake on the drafting board. Maybe her ability to seek out design solutions might disappear. Perhaps her cognitive abilities would deteriorate to where she would stare blankly at you if you asked her a pointed question requiring more than a yes or no answer.

One weekend when Sally was with her school friends in Hyde Park, I told Alice I was worried her drinking was far past anything recreational, or remotely social. It was no longer that she simply enjoyed a drink in the evening. It was rather that she had to have it, her body demanded it, and alcohol had become an addiction.

I used those words, and she shouted back at me. "Who the hell are you to tell me what I can or can't do? I will do whatever pleases me. You seem to have no trouble doing that. It's always you first, isn't it?"

The earlier sweetness in her manner that drew me to her had somehow dissolved. She was either anxious, depressed or angry and moved through those emotions without much warning.

"Will you talk to someone, Alice? I'm worried about you."

"Some therapist. You think that will help me?"

"Maybe. I will go with you. You pick somebody, anybody."

Her eyes were wild with anger: "I'm so sick of your shit, I can't stand it. You choose."

I did choose. I called some friends and asked around. Finally, we found someone whose specialty was addiction. He had been a drug abuser and alcoholic himself. Now with graduate training he was a counselor. His record of helping people was impressive; it was a mysterious balance between tough love, and Jungian analysis.

At our first meeting downtown, we sat in his office and made small talk, until he asked, "Why are you here?"

To that, I told him what I thought and believed about Alice and what I saw as a mounting problem.

"I don't think I have a drinking problem." Alice said to him to deflect the direction of the conversation.

"And why is that?" he countered.

She explained that she enjoyed a drink after dinner, and sometimes had two, which was no big deal.

"Or three or four," I suggested. "And that's a big deal."

"If you don't think you have a problem with alcohol, or can't admit that, I can't help you," he said softly, looking directly at her.

I started to answer, but he held up his hand to stop me, "Let her speak."

"First of all, I don't know why I'm here, it seems silly," she said.

"You don't honestly know why the three of us are talking about you?" he went on. "Alice, you're an architect and a writer, obviously a smart woman. That can't be true."

"This is bullshit," she burst out. "I have a few drinks, and this guy thinks I'm a drunk."

The therapist took a deep breath and folded his hands together on his lap. He said we could come to the problem from a different perspective.

"Let me ask you this: Are you happy in your relationship with this man?" he said, pointing to me.

"Mostly not," she answered. "It's been better."

Wisely, the therapist shook his head to acknowledge what she had said. "When did it take a turn for the worse?"

"I didn't say it's awful, I said it could be better."

The therapist quickly wrote something down on the pad on the table next to him and put it aside.

"Do you drink because you're unhappy with him?" he inquired further.

"Sometimes yes. But, there are other things. Look, I don't drink because of him. I had a life I didn't like before I ever laid eyes on him. He only adds to it with his manipulation, and phoniness."

"I want this to be a safe place for both of you," the therapist said. "There are no right or wrong answers, and you both deserve to feel how you do. You want to make this work, or don't you?"

He stood up and asked, "Can we continue later?" Our session was over.

'Sure," Alice said, "Maybe we can fix this."

With that, the therapist turned to me, "What do you think?"

I told him I was willing to return and talk, or if Alice wanted to see him alone, that was fine with me too.

He nodded, "My recommendation is that the three of us meet again. Let's see what we can learn from the process, talking. I'm sure the more we get everything out in the open, your feelings, the easier things will be."

We continued to see the therapist who I genuinely liked, and Alice somehow tolerated. It wasn't until our third meeting that she told him what she didn't like about me. I was distant and only gave her what was safe for me, so she didn't get much. She told him I came from a mess of a family, which was true, mental illness, abuse, and alcoholism. She said I spent most of the time since then trying to protect myself from people. We had no intimacy and that all the sweet words and softness were a

74

smokescreen to keep people out. I needed distance to feel safe. She was tired of it. She had had enough of warmed-over emotions; she wanted the real thing.

With a pinched face, she continued: "Sometimes I feel like he just wanted someone to take care of Sally, that's it. If he got sex or a real relationship as well, that came as a bonus. We live in a house of cards."

I told the therapist I didn't dispute the distance I created. Anyone with common sense would in a family such as mine where nowhere was safe, trust didn't exist.

"You both require a safe place. Stop the overthinking, the manipulation. Let your feelings determine how you behave. If you are angry with her, tell Alice that. And you tell him as well, Alice. Do not hide or mask behaviors; it is all fair. Put it on the table."

From the sessions, I got some clarity though Alice was mute with her feelings after therapy. The drinking slowed down for a month, but then it picked up again. She was unashamed about the amount she drank. Her health got worse, and inertia took over her. Thoughts of any kind of future, professionally or personally stopped.

It was now spring in Chicago, and I opened all the living room windows as I prepared our Saturday fish dish. I had been to the fishmonger earlier and came back with sea scallops, grouper and lobster tails. My intention was to make a classic seafood risotto.

I cleaned the meat from a pound and a half lobster and shredded it into big chunks. I added a filet of fresh grouper, and a pound of large scallops, putting it all in the refrigerator. I measured a cup of Italian Arborio rice and three cups of chicken stock, two shallots, unsalted butter, chives, lemon zest and half a cup of Brut Champagne.

I started the risotto by melting the butter, adding the shallots, and sautéing them until soft. I slowly added the rice with a half cup of the stock mixture. I added another half-cup every few minutes, and stirred until the liquid was absorbed. It required about forty minutes to finish. It took five minutes to cook the grouper and scallops and the lobster in a buttered pan.

I took the cooked rice off the heat and gently folded in the hot grouper and scallops until it was thoroughly mixed. Last came grated

Parmigiano cheese on top. In the center of the dish, I put the lobster meat and fresh parsley in a colorful circle.

That seafood risotto extravaganza got rave reviews at our townhouse table. It was presented with a mixed green salad with scallions, and the familiar mustard vinaigrette.

We ate well, but otherwise not much of import was happening in our lives. Alice stopped writing at night. However, she was staying up reading women's romance novels, which she hitherto called trash. Whatever ambition she entertained pretty much vanished. She seemed to waste much of the day. Even her numerous errands seemed to constrict, and the only time she went out was to the butcher and the supermarket. Grudgingly she made uninspired meals, and each Wednesday we went around the corner to the taco shop.

Sally being self-absorbed as teenagers usually are noticed nothing out of the ordinary until one day when the two of us were home alone.

She asked, "What's up with Alice? She doesn't seem to want to do anything anymore. I don't get it."

For the past few months, every other weekend Sally was staying with different school friends in Hyde Park. She hadn't paid any attention to us, or so I thought.

"I think she needs time to prepare herself for the next chapter in her life, that's all. She was an architect for all those years. Now she has the challenge of being a writer. It's a hard transition, a bit scary."

Nodding her head in understanding, she soon was upstairs on her phone with friends.

As the warm weather came, we got invitations to go to a friend's lake home in Wisconsin. It was the one place Alice felt comfortable. She could sit around and do crossword puzzles, and read trashy novels, and drink. Nobody paid attention, they were too busy.

Although Alice's friend Ann did corner me one afternoon when Alice was in the lake swimming which she rarely did.

"Alice is acting strange these days, what's wrong?" the woman said with concern.

"I wish I knew," I told her. "My guess is that the next chapter of her life with the writing is a bit fearful. You have to put yourself out there and be rejected before things go right. That's scary for anybody."

"Oh God," she suggested, "I couldn't go back to college, and do something entirely different with my life. I'd be petrified."

"It's the newness, and uncertainty that you'll do well, that kind of thing."

"She's got more courage than I do," the woman admitted. As she was about to add something else her husband called to her from the lakeside.

Alice toyed with going back to architecture and turning her back on the writing. The subject of Stanford didn't come up as if it had never happened.

I started to blame myself for what was happening to her. I already had one failed marriage, why couldn't it be two. The habit I fashioned in that coal town family had been to be untruthful to myself. It was because examining the hidden parts of my own psyche was too painful. To try to save Alice I went to talk with the therapist by myself. I didn't tell her. Perhaps I was too ashamed, and it meant my own culpability.

In his office alone, he didn't ask me why I was there. He simply said, "You want to talk about something without Alice in the room?"

"Yes," I answered with a look of guilt on my face.

"What is it?" he prodded though his tone was gentle.

I told him it seemed to me that I didn't give her enough of me, emotionally.

"And why do you think that is?" he continued.

"Because I'm afraid, that's why."

He cleared his throat, walked to his desk in the far corner, and brought a pencil and notebook over to where we were sitting.

"Can you explain why?" he inquired.

With a nervous laugh, I told him that I had been frightened as a small child, afraid to show anybody my feelings. My father had hit me once for my openness. After that, I closed as a defense for a lifetime, and only ever let my feelings remain at the most superficial level to protect myself.

"You give Alice just enough to not starve. Put her on this diet of bread and water. With that, you're in control, and not vulnerable to being hurt. Does that sum up what you've told me?"

"Yeah, and I owe her more," I added.

"You certainly do. Otherwise, that's cruel."

I looked at him and nodded and stared at the floor in embarrassment. He said that if I loved her, I was going to have to change my behavior toward her right away. Because to him, the relationship was falling apart.

He held up an index finger in warning. "That's not to say that Alice doesn't have issues. She does. If you see alcohol as an obstacle, it probably is. My guess is that she cannot stop her drinking; it's spiraling out of control. She's on a collision course, and it won't be pretty."

He got up from his chair, walked over to the single window in the office, and looked down at the street. He turned to me.

"Let me give you some advice. You believe you can stop her from drinking and lean on her to quit. I am a recovering alcoholic, and I am telling you it won't work. Persuade, or threaten, it is all the same. Useless. Until that person hits bottom, and only then, can they start to climb out of that hole."

I held my palms up in the air in frustration to what he had said. Did I believe him?

He smiled and leaned in closer to me. "What you can do is work on trust, more honesty. Be vulnerable to Alice and show that side to her. She'll meet you halfway."

"But..." I exclaimed uncertain.

"If Alice is an alcoholic, she's an alcoholic. You can't change that. She has to come to grips with it. It appears she hasn't. It doesn't matter how she got there. There could be many factors. It wasn't you that caused the problem, that's for certain."

After he had finished speaking, he looked at his wristwatch, and said we were done for the day. "If you want to do this again, call me."

I handed him a hundred dollar check I had stashed in my shirt pocket, said my goodbyes, and walked out the door.

For some unknown reason I didn't call him again. It was as if he had told me all that I needed to know in those fifty minutes. It wasn't me who made Alice this way. Something or someone else triggered it.

We saw him two more times as a couple. Then Alice complained that she had had enough of his sanctimonious blather, so we stopped.

During this time, an author friend found Alice an intern position at a literary agency. She spent two afternoons each week reading slush pile book manuscripts and answering the phone. It was a one-woman office with maybe twenty authors represented, and Alice loved the place.

In fact, after only a month there, the woman gave Alice an assignment to edit one of her client's new books. It was a new handbook on searching out genealogies. With enthusiasm, Alice spent three weeks and countless hours with it and turned out a flawless edit. Two days turned into four days per week. Before long, Alice was getting a small cash stipend as well as learning the in-and-outs of big-time publishing.

Alice got another editing assignment, and for some unknown reason just sat on it. She let time and deadlines pass to the point that the agent pulled the project. From then on, the relationship cooled, and eventually ended. They stopped talking.

I never questioned Alice why she'd ignored the book assignment and let it linger. She had spent her entire professional life working under impossible deadlines with developers and contractors screaming for results. She never bent for a second, working long hours into the night huddled over a drafting table. Once the literary agency job vanished, Alice slipped back into herself. If I made suggestions, she would just snap at me.

CATFISH

I had a wildlife photographer friend call her and invite her to write an article on Canada's Arctic for National Geographic. He would do the photos. When I asked her about it, she told me that he was too difficult to work with, and the Arctic had no interest for her.

I believe it was at that point I stopped trying to fix Alice and ignored her drinking. I would slowly attempt to repair what was wrong with me. I had the ability to make those changes. To recognize what no longer served me. And if I could or should do something about them. But would I, or could I follow through and admit what needed to be confronted, and change it? What had supposedly protected a twelve-year-old frightened boy may not do the same for a fifty-four-year-old man any longer.

Now, if I didn't like something with Alice's and my life, I tried to speak up about it truthfully and not attempt to manipulate the outcome. I wanted to make an honest try at resolution, once we identified the issue, whatever it was. It was easy to see that her drinking was the eight-hundred-pound gorilla sitting next to us on the couch. We never talked about it and if we did, it was only in anger and frustration on my part.

The therapist was right, only Alice could identify its scourge, and admit that it was careening out of control. The result was predictable. An imploding marriage.

Yet I believed against all the odds that much of our trouble, this distance, came from me. It was a hidden fear of being hurt, which had been there since childhood, always lurking.

Usually, the way I reacted was to try to figure out what someone wanted. Then I would endeavor to give it to them, or enough of it, whatever it was, so they would leave me alone. Not literally alone, though enough to make fewer demands upon me.

That meant I would hug Alice when I came into the house. Only because that was what I thought she expected of me. Quite a natural reaction for anybody, or was it? Although, it was not what I really wanted. Instead, it was to placate her, to provide enough affection to quiet her. Was it wrong to think that way? Yes, I am certain it was wrong and misguided.

How could I be more open, available to her, or others? What did I need to do? Should I start by confessing all my inner most fears to her? I thought, yes. Yet how could that achieve anything but a woman's contempt for a man. Especially one whom she was told to believe was stoic, strong and protective, concealing his weaknesses.

Years before, I had been in a Zen Buddhist men's group, and the biggest complaint from these assembled middle-aged men was they felt disrespected once they opened up. They were viewed as weaklings. Those revelations had the opposite effect to what they had wanted. They encountered women's contempt. Once contempt came, it never left. Maybe that was what I was afraid of with Alice.

Having Alice next to me in and out of bed felt so secure, and right. There was this genuine niceness about her that I had never encountered before. Maybe some women were more physically attractive at that young age, though once you scratched the surface nothing was there. You could not talk about anything meaningful, really. Everything moved in a superficial circle, which maybe the youthfulness of two thirty-something people might somehow explain. With Alice, it was different. She had depth.

Excessive drinking or not, I wanted it to last, last forever. I had no plans to walk away because it was infuriating or uncomfortable. What if she had developed cancer like a friend's young wife had. Was he going to say, "I've had enough trips to the hospital for your chemotherapy drips. Let's go to Vegas instead. Put this all behind us."

The situation called for a fight within me, and I wrestled with whether I could wage war against myself. Alice was becoming a drunk. I had to face that fact. The first step was to stop my own drinking and set an example.

However, when I suggested it to the therapist, he had only laughed. "Stop with the best intentions stuff. It's pointless to an alcoholic. They simply do not care, no matter how agreeable they appear. It's a dead end. I've been down that road with a lot of people."

I picked a night and didn't drink a whiskey with her. No wine was on the table, so I avoided that temptation. I did the same thing the next night, and the one after that.

At this point, she could recognize what I was attempting to do. "You've stopped drinking, huh?" Alice said holding her first scotch of the night. "Is this your way of taking the high moral ground to teach me a lesson?"

"No," I answered which was false.

"I see what you're up to," she almost hissed at me. "You think you'll shame me into not drinking. Why don't you just come out and say you don't like my drinking?"

"Okay, I'll say it," but I didn't.

"Get it out," she urged with anger in her tone.

With a long sigh, I told her that I thought both our drinking habits had gotten to the point that it wasn't healthy for either of us.

"Listen," she said with no disguise of the anger in her voice. "You can't take away my freedom. I won't let you."

I shook my head no. "What I want is for you to stop the self-destructive behavior. The drinking has become a problem."

"And you're judging me?" she screamed out. Fortunately, Sally was in Hyde Park with friends. It seemed that she was doing more and more of that perhaps to stay out of the house.

"We'll both take a break and support each other."

"Where did you get that idea? Did you talk to that dumb therapist? He probably put you up to it. That's the way it sounds to me."

"This is insane. We're arguing all the time. I think the booze makes it worse."

She stood up and started for the stairs still holding her drink. She called me an asshole as she mounted the steps to the bedroom for escape.

When Saturday came, Alice had to go to the university to file paperwork that would allow her degree to be granted in the next semester. She continued to do essay grading for her primary professor whom she always liked and had sponsored her research in San Diego.

Saturday meant fish. I noticed my Chicago fishmonger had fresh-caught catfish from Mississippi in the display case. I got three large fillets for dinner. It had been a long time since I'd eaten catfish. It was a favorite of Sally's late grandfather, Tucker, who had grown up along the Yazoo River. He caught catfish for his entire childhood. Folks called the river,

The Yellow Dog, because it had taken on the color of the yellow clay soils of the banks.

In preparing catfish southern Mississippi style, he taught me you always fry it in very hot peanut oil for about 3-4 minutes. Use a cast iron pan. First, he marinated the catfish in buttermilk, which I did for at least a half hour. Once marinated, dust it with white corn meal (it must be white, he always insisted) and add two tablespoons of a spicy seafood mix like Zatarain's. It had to be a New Orleans brand, unless you had a grandmother around who remembered 1920. He insisted you needed a dipping sauce for the catfish too. His sauce recipe was two cups of Duke's mayonnaise, a cup of chopped bread and butter pickles, spring onion tips, two tablespoons of finely chopped garlic, lemon juice and zest, tabasco and Worcestershire, and two ounces of Jack Daniels whiskey. He said it was crucial to dry the fried catfish fillet for about 20-30 seconds on a paper towel to absorb the excess oil before serving.

I added a baked beet salad with hazelnut oil and scallions to accompany the catfish for dinner. Sally particularly loved the catfish because she remembered Tucker making a big deal of it during the summers at his lake house. He always gave her some small task to perform.

When Alice wasn't at home doing little but thinking and looking off into space, she found things to do at the university. Her advisor arranged for her to teach an undergraduate summer course on creative writing. Naturally, she threw herself into it, re-reading the leading Twentieth Century authors, and adding a handful of well-regarded contemporary fiction, most of whom were women.

She taught two classes a week. On Fridays, the class broke up into groups to examine student writing. It was always lively. The last week or final for the course was preparation of a two-thousand-word short story. That represented half of the term grade.

Alice blossomed during this class. She started smiling again and spent early evening reading student stories. She often shared what they wrote with me.

There was a Puerto Rican woman she adored whose stories were well written but full of expletives and anger at her abusive upbringing.

"I think she's the best writer in the class," she hinted, "but she uses 'fuck' too much and it spoils her stories."

"Then give her a heads-up, tell her to clean up the language," I suggested.

Alice shook her head no. "If I do that, she'll shut down, and it'll go all downhill."

"Have coffee with her and praise her work which you like anyway. Ease into the criticism."

"Maybe I'll do that," she said.

She met with the student, and the mentor role seemed to work. It wasn't so much criticism as much as suggestion. It seemed to produce cleaner, better thought-out writing without losing the underlying energy. Alice was pleased.

I told her that teaching college might be a career path she would enjoy. "You get a couple of classes a semester, and summers off. Not a bad way to go through life."

"The money stinks," she said, "Everybody's an adjunct, part-time."

"Well, we're doing fine. You have that window if you want. Your professors respect you; they'll help you get hired, I'm sure."

She said she wasn't fit for teaching; it would become a bore after a while. Working for a magazine would not. Each assignment would be different, a real challenge.

"Call Dan. He does ten big assignments a year for magazines with different writers."

"Gawd no. When he is around me, he's always staring at my tits. I can't work with him. Anyway, I don't care about polar bears or caribou."

I laughed. I believed what she said rang true. Despite having a wife and two children, he was a notorious womanizer and had numerous affairs.

There were other magazine opportunities. Professional journals and magazines like Architectural Record or House Beautiful, where being an architect held some cache.

RAINBOW TROUT

The summer class ended and one of the department faculty asked if she wanted to pursue a doctorate. Once that was done, she would be fulltime faculty and easily get tenure. She could do it right there at the same university and continue teaching the whole time.

It seemed that job security rated low on Alice's list. She planned to ride out the freelance world with whatever writing she could find. She might do book editing to pay the bills, or even the summer teaching. In the end, she didn't pursue it.

Her drinking continued and worsened. I became more vocal in my objections, telling her to slow down. That remark would naturally spawn an argument, but nothing changed. Week after week, she was walking around with ever darkening circles under her lovely brown eyes. I'd lost the game. Things weren't getting better, and my threats became useless, they didn't work. In desperation, I said we might see the therapist again, and she laughed.

"That charlatan," she said with a sinister smile, "What does he know?"

I once had a house on the McKenzie River in central Oregon. The river was about thirty miles outside of Eugene and fed by the melting snows from the Cascade Mountains. Its freezing waters had some of the world's best trout though quite small. Usually, two trout might provide enough meat to satisfy a hungry man.

For the few summers I used the house, mostly living there alone, I would fly fish in the early morning or at dusk. I always caught three or four trout that I'd cook. I would set up a small grill at the side of the house and drink a cold beer as I watched the trout take on a flaky consistency and burned the flesh enough to have a crispy taste.

On my weekend visit to the fishmonger, I spotted some rainbow trout in the case. A card claimed they were from the Pacific Northwest, and to me, that meant Oregon. Without losing any time since there were so few of them displayed, I bought four trout that weighed a little under two pounds each. That meant we would get a pound, or close to it, of the sweet flesh to eat from each of the fish.

Since they had to be grilled, I set up the small Weber grill we had on the back porch under the El tracks. I laid enough charcoal briquettes for a decent fire and had a bag of Maplewood to use for flavoring.

The thing with fresh trout is you need an almost burnt exterior, and then the fun begins. You peel off the dried skin and slowly begin the de-boning process. You need to be careful extracting the succulent white flesh, because the trout bones are tiny and easy to miss.

An enthusiastic bite can easily result in a miniscule bone in your throat, which you're lucky to dislodge. If you don't, it could remain there for days until your food finally pushes it into your stomach. If it doesn't, that may require an uncomfortable visit to an Emergency Room.

I'm convinced the truest way to grill trout is with a tiny amount of butter melted on each fish. At the last minute, squeeze the juice from a lemon over it. That's the way I prepared them and served them with head and eyes to Sally and Alice.

Slowly with my knife and fingers, I removed the dry trout skin, which sloughed off easily exposing the white flesh. I grabbed the backbone at the tail and pulled it toward the head exposing a labyrinth of translucent spines. I dislodged it and put the backbone on an empty plate I had for that purpose. Once done, I returned to the pile of white fish on my plate and took the tines of my fork through it to uncover any other bones I might have missed, and there were some.

"Is this worth all that trouble?" Alice complained while Sally made a face of impatience.

I handed the cleaned trout to Alice and told her she might want to add a bit more butter. Then I started on the next and handed it to Sally.

"It's very tasty," Alice volunteered after her first bite, and forced a smile.

Sally was in the middle of chewing a forkful of trout, and she let out a groan, pulling this long thin bone out of her mouth. "Gross," she added, as she put it on the bone pile.

"It really is the best of freshwater fish, but the small bones are hell. It's so easy to get one stuck in your throat."

The last trout sat there in its isolation on the plate, and nobody reached for it.

Alice teased me about Oregon, the house, and fishing, saying that it was more fun to catch the trout than eat it.

"Well, for such a small fish, they put up quite a fight in the water. That's where the fun is," I added as I finished my plate.

I missed the Oregon house as a getaway and wished I hadn't sold it. I didn't have the cash to keep a house that I might visit two or three weeks a year. I had considered it until I encountered a string of burglaries from the desperate druggies who occupied some of the river valley. If you weren't there to watch it, someone would burn it down. However, the irony came three years after I sold it and returned to Chicago.

Oregon is always dry in the summer and fall. A small fire on a Christmas tree farm in the McKenzie Valley burned most of the houses for sixty miles until you reached the foothills of the Cascades. It was devastating, though there was little loss of life. I was told later that my old house burned to the ground in twenty minutes

Those summers were the only time I fished to eat. I could count on a stringer of fish for the grill on most weekends. The river itself was too cold for swimming and not terribly deep. However, it was one of America's finest trout rivers.

I remember eating at one of the few cafes in the valley when I first got the house. I noticed on the wall of the restaurant, an old newspaper clipping from the early 1930s that quoted President Herbert Hoover. He said, "The McKenzie is my favorite river in the whole country." That was their claim to fame, I imagine. The entire country was out of work during those Depression years, and nobody had time to fish except Hoover. Hoover was probably our least popular modern President if you don't count Nixon. However, he certainly knew a thing or two about trout.

Things continued as before. Melancholy took over Alice who lost interest in most everything including bringing an Italian cuisine spin to weekdays.

Sally was doing very well at the University of Chicago academically. Since most of her classmates were children of the faculty, they tended to live in the neighborhood around the school. And every other weekend might be a sleepover for a night.

As the weather got warmer there were more school social events including dances. One evening as I was half-asleep on the couch, I got a call from the school.

After identifying myself as Sally's father, the voice insisted that I come immediately to Hyde Park to deal with this. What, I asked? A stern male voice announced, "You'd better get down here right away."

"Is she hurt?" I asked with some fearfulness.

"No, it's not that. But I'd advise you to come as soon as possible."

I told Alice about the call, and she asked me if I wanted her along. I said it was probably better for me to see what's wrong in the first place. Driving on Lake Shore drive, I was very close to speeding for the twenty-five minutes it took me to get to the university. Sally had been at a dance at Mandel Hall, and after looking at a couple of gothic buildings and asking a bored student, I found it.

As soon as I walked into the building, I noticed one of her classmates asleep or passed out on a bench in the foyer. Beth Watkins, whose father was a professor of Sanskrit seemed to be unconscious though still making moaning sounds as if she were in pain. Inside the large hall, a forty-something teacher met me, and asked me my name, and then pulled me to the side.

"What's wrong? I asked nervously, "Is Sally alright?" Thinking maybe, she had gone out to sneak a cigarette the way kids do and had been assaulted.

"Well," announced, "she violated school policy and was found with an open can of beer in the hallway. Teenage drinking is a serious offense at this school, and we have zero tolerance."

Apparently, one of her girlfriends who lived in the nearby neighborhood had purchased, or someone else had for her, a six-pack of beer. Ten girls had been drinking it and Sally was the one who had been caught drinking from a can.

"Please take Sally home," the teacher-monitor suggested. "Tomorrow the headmaster will call you for a meeting to discuss this, and what disciplinary measures the school plans to take with her."

Sally and I drove home mostly in dead silence. In the dark, she couldn't see the smile I had on my face. After all, I had expected the worst, and this was simply adolescent risk-taking, and seemingly harmless.

Inside the house, Sally went upstairs to bed without a word to Alice. I explained to Alice what had happened at the school dance.

"Is that all it is?" Alice said and started laughing. "Two sips of beer and you're busted. I guess that's it for Miss Perfect."

Smiling and relieved, I shook my head in agreement.

At ten o'clock, the next morning the headmaster promptly called. She told me the school had decided to suspend Sally from classes for one day for the offense. She did not expect the behavior to be repeated.

All that next day Sally sulked around the house. She spent most of the day on the telephone with her girlfriends who had been involved. Her popularity at the school increased, because now she had the reputation as someone who did not 'rat out' their friends. That was big. Even the boys were impressed at her courage.

"Does Sally drink?" Alice had asked me when we were alone. "I think this is a one-off, you know the excitement of the dance, and all that teenage stuff."

"She never has wine at dinner, that I remember," Alice went on. "But I didn't tell you, I found a half a pack of cigarettes on the floor near the washer-dryer. It must have fallen out of her pocket."

Looking at Alice I made an exaggerated grimace, "Well, it's those years we all went through."

"Yep," Alice said, and went back to the book she had been reading in bed.

Business picked up for me. I found myself traveling to San Francisco several times a month to meet with Chevron. I once went to Paris for three days to confer with Roussel, a French drug giant on US acquisitions. Then right after that, I was sent to Brazil for two weeks to work on a joint venture opportunity for a Dallas company.

Alice stepped in with the day-to-day responsibilities with Sally, which pretty much consisted of making sure her clothes were clean, and she had a small breakfast and healthy dinner a couple times a week. The bond between the two became a strong mother and daughter relationship. It was a substitute for the missing one with Sally's own mother who was absent from her life. Joyce pushed her aside for the little she did for her daughter. I imagine Sally felt that abandonment at some level.

After the time in South America, Chevron asked me to come to San Francisco again to discuss acquisitions. Alice said she wanted to tag along. Maybe she would take another look at Stanford. It seemed like fun. We arranged for Sally to spend the weekend with her close Hyde Park friend, Monica Sitwell, whom I knew well. She had stayed over at our house on two or three occasions. I also liked Monica's mother who was among the friendlier university types.

We flew to San Francisco and stayed at the St. Francis Hotel on Union Square. Chevron's headquarters was maybe six blocks away on Market Street downtown. It was a convenient spot for restaurants and stores, and we could get on the interstate quickly for the Palo Alto drive.

For some inexplicable reason Alice decided to forget the Stanford visit. We just enjoyed the city taking the cable car to the wharf and eating at some dive in Chinatown.

"I could live here," she said at one of the North Beach cafes. "It's small enough and doesn't intimate you like Chicago does. And I could write here too. The place makes me want to write."

That remark came as a surprise. Although, I figured it was much like me sitting in Paris last month in the middle of the French spring believing I could live there. I would take on a Gallic manner, and conduct international business, or maybe write instead.

"Let's move here," Alice said to me over dinner at a waterfront fish restaurant. "Sally could spent her last year in Memphis. Then she's off to college somewhere."

"Are you serious?" I asked Alice uncertain.

"I am," she answered, and rubbed her fingers through her short dark hair. She leaned forward on the table for emphasis and spoke.

"What she really wants, she told me, was to spend her last year of school with her grandmother who's getting frail. Joyce would put her in the same episcopal girl's school. That was Sally's plan not mine."

"Oh," I exclaimed, thinking that I had been missing things in everybody's life.

Alice said with sadness in her tone, "I need a change, and I'm not sure what. Nothing interests me anymore."

"Change, huh?" I whispered.

"Yeah," she said, and then dropped the subject.

YELLOW FIN TUNA and ZUPPA di PESCI

Back in Chicago, the week passed without incident or further mention of Memphis or San Francisco. When Saturday rolled around, I headed for the fish purveyor as usual. At the store, I scored some rather nice yellow fin tuna. It had been caught in Baja California and made its way to Chicago.

Alone in the kitchen, I cut the tuna into small steaks and put it in the fridge. Next, I began to make a sauce. I added two tablespoons of soy sauce, and sesame oil, honey and kosher salt to taste. I sliced up a single green onion, and toasted sesame seeds. Then, I added a generous pinch of cayenne. Once the sauce was complete, I marinated the tuna in the mixture for about an hour, turning the steaks once.

On the stove, I drizzled a little olive oil in my trusty cast iron pan and turned the burners up to high heat. I removed the yellow fin tuna from the marinate and cooked them for two minutes on each side, timing it carefully.

When the tuna was finished, I laid them on a cutting board and coated them with what was left of the toasted sesame seeds on each side. I took a half of a fresh lime and squeezed the juice on the fish.

The tuna steaks were placed on a bed of brown rice and garnished with fresh parsley. I dribbled the soy and sesame sauce generously over each seared purple morsel. Everything looked and tasted wonderful. Both Alice and Sally kept adding a spoonful of the sesame sauce until the dish was empty. Much lip smacking went on.

To cleanse the palate, I presented them with a Wasabi sorbet. I had picked it up in a downtown Asian market along with the authentic soy sauce. It was too foreign for Sally, but Alice ate every bite.

Alice could not let go of the San Francisco attraction. She blamed Chicago for whatever was bothering her. She told me repeatedly she needed to change her geography, or she would die. This city which represented her childhood, education and career had taken on the blame for what was happening to her. What was it? I would ask. For someone so intelligent and articulate, she couldn't explain it. Was it the air, the people, the winters? What had brought her to this standstill?

Then something happened. I was going on a trip to the East Coast and planned to be gone for three days, first to Princeton and then Philadelphia. It was very early summer, and Sally had another week of school at the university. She had already left the house catching her ride with a girlfriend who lived on the Northside.

I had ordered a taxi to O'Hare. For some reason it took longer this time for one to show up. We were standing on the front porch in the morning sunshine. Alice returned inside to get a second cup of coffee. Remembering some missing papers I needed for the trip, I had left the door ajar for a few seconds and hurried into the TV room where they sat on a coffee table. Together we met on the porch again just as the cab arrived, and Alice kissed me goodbye. In a moment, the taxi started for the airport and Alice went back inside, putting down her coffee and starting upstairs.

When she walked into our bedroom, Alice was shocked to see a young Black man stuffing her jewelry hurriedly into his pockets. Alice let out a scream. He quickly turned toward her, pushing her out of the doorway and down the stairs, as he bounded out of the front door into the street.

She was more frightened than hurt, cutting her cheek as she fell against the exposed brick wall along the staircase. She touched the wound and there was a little blood. Feeling faint, she sat on the steps and caught her breath. It was several minutes before she was herself again. Her first call was to the police, and a squad car was there within several minutes. Two cops talked to her about the incident, and she made a report of the stolen items, which included her favorite string of pearls. She gave them a vague description of the man, which could fit most anyone walking the streets of Chicago.

Next, she called a girlfriend who was at home and drove over to calm her down after the ordeal. She asked her friend if she could borrow her large dog, and that evening the woman's husband returned with their Black lab mix. Meanwhile Sally returned from school and learned what had happened, and it upset her too.

It was the next evening before Alice called and told me what had happened. I told her I would cut the trip short, but she insisted there was no need. By the time I got home three days later, the robbery had convinced Alice it was time to move to San Francisco.

Change didn't bother me, and if a California move would stop her excessive drinking, then I would wholeheartedly agree. It didn't matter to me.

So, that's what we did. Sally was going to be spending the next school year with Joyce in Memphis. Sally was enthusiastic about it. She had been thinking about a small university in Dallas. She wanted to be with Joyce before she really got too sick. We turned our gaze westward.

Alice had forgotten to submit some form to the university that was an administrative requirement. Now she would have to wait for the January graduation cycle to get her master's.

My consulting business was portable. I only had one client in Chicago, the rest were on the Eastern Seaboard, or in California, namely Chevron. Moving would be easy.

With Sally in Memphis that summer, we could make as many exploratory trips to California as we wished or change our minds and remain in Chicago. Wherever we lived, Sally would visit us during college breaks, and for holidays. She was a young woman now, and fiercely independent.

When Saturday came around, I made my usual trip to the Chicago Fish House and decided upon a Sicilian seafood stew, Zuppa di Pesci. Saddened a bit by Sally's departure, I hurried to find what I needed. I bought two whole Pollocks, a pound of monkfish, shrimp, three whole langoustines, mussels and two squid.

Home alone while Alice was in the suburbs visiting friends, I had the kitchen to myself. It was a relief. I had gone through an emotional roller coaster lately.

I started by peeling the shrimp and sautéed the shells to begin the stock. Once done I added onions and fennel, and parsley stems. When that cooked, I threw in garlic and waited twenty seconds for its scent to tell me it was done. Then I added thick Roma tomatoes, a pinch of cinnamon and water to thin out the stock.

Next went in the chopped squid, the monkfish, shrimp, langoustines and the whole Pollocks with heads. I cooked the seafood mixture until the Pollocks were soft and removed them. I then added the mussels to add liquid and flavor. Next I took the Pollock meat off the bones and laid it on top of the seafood. I covered the pot and cooked it for another fifteen minutes.

It was perfect, and Alice loved it although her forbearers hailed from Genoa in the North. There was plenty of freshly baked bread for dipping, which truthfully, I enjoyed more than the seafood itself.
With Sally spending most of the summer at Joyce's lake place an hour from Memphis, Alice pushed to make a real San Francisco exploratory trip.

We flew into SFO, rented a mustang convertible, and headed into the city. We parked in a lot in North Beach and made Russian Hill our first target. We found two apartments for rent in the local newspaper. The first one was spacious but there was an electric pole with thick wires outside the living room picture window.

The second apartment we saw was in an enclosed courtyard garden. Inside its many windows provided a panoramic view of the Bay over the squat buildings of Fisherman's wharf. A Chinese man showed us around. When he answered questions, we looked at one another trying to understand what he had said. After the tour, he gave us the owner's business card. The owner was a lawyer downtown on Columbus Avenue across from the triangular Transamerica tower.

It was a short walk to Chinatown from the Russian Hill apartment, and we stopped at a crowded restaurant on Grant Street that looked interesting.

"What do you think?" I asked Alice and she smiled at me.

"My guess is that apartment with the courtyard was built right after the great fire, maybe in 1907, around that time. Did you notice the inlaid stone tiles in the hallway? Beautiful touch."

"No, I missed that," I admitted.

"The picture windows all had lead frames and open with a side crank. It's a feature left over from early Twentieth Century homes. An architect designed it; you can see the quality everywhere you look. The first place we looked at was some builder's quick makeover."

"You saw all that," I said, surprised.

"We can afford it, right?" she asked her hands on top of each other in some sort of supplication.

I looked at the ad listing in the newspaper we'd circled, and said yes, it's doable.

"Well, are you ready to take the plunge?"

It was a little fast for me to react. I hesitated for a moment, which she sensed.

"So, you don't want to do this. It was all talk." Now she folded her arms and leaned back in the chair, a smirk on her face.

"You know if we do this, you leave a lot behind. We don't know this place. We're just tourists. Chicago, we know like the back of our hand."

"I'm bored with Chicago; I want a change. Look, I desperately need this. Do you understand?"

"Alright, let's give it a try. I'll call the owner, and tell him we want it," which is exactly what I did before dessert.

That night as Alice drifted off to sleep; I remained awake and wondered if I had made the right choice. The next morning, we signed a lease, and I wrote a check. We had a showcase apartment on the Crooked Street, Lombard.

At lunch, Alice called Sally and told her what we had done. I could hear Sally on the other end, say, "Oh my God, you're totally crazy."

On the long flight back, Alice fell asleep. I kept whispering to myself, "What have you done?" I said it repeatedly because there was uncertainty lodged in my stomach.

We had two weeks to move, and it went fast. A moving van unloaded our townhouse furniture and clothes when I was in Philadelphia on business. Alice was an architect, so when I stepped into the apartment everything was already in its rightful place. As always, there were fresh gladiolas in a vase on the dining room table.

Within a month, the newness had worn off and Alice seemed glued to the apartment. She seemed afraid to venture out except for the grocery store. The evenings we walked down the hill to a North Beach Italian restaurant. She soon tired of that so we would sit in front of a fire and watch the fog envelope the city. Sometimes we would talk, sometimes we didn't, but there was always drinking. It seemed more than ever and now I would join her out of sheer frustration.

We had a dinner together most evenings and drinks to fill the empty night. I'd talk about work which had slowed, and she would talk about things she wanted to accomplish though never did. The inertia fed on itself. We had no real friends here. Occasionally we might dine with the friendly lawyer landlord who lived above us. Sometimes I might have a client in town for the evening and we'd take them to North Beach for dinner. Twice she joined me, and afterward begged off for future dinners.

"You go," she'd say defensively, "I'm not very good company."

After finishing her memoir, Alice started a new project. It was a novel about a Chicago architect. Her adventures included solving crimes in the city. It was out of her usual genre, but I liked the idea and encouraged her to finish the book. Midway through, after several months of working on it, she threw the manuscript aside, calling it childish nonsense.

I told her: "People write crime novels, it's what fills the airport bookstores along with romance novels. They sell more books than all the rest combined."

"I couldn't write that women's romance crap," she announced. "At least the other stuff has dead bodies." She laughed aloud at what she had said.

"Try the crime thing with Chicago; you know the city and its corruption. It's a murder capitol, c'mon," I advised.

"Did you know we bribed a commissioner for a city job? Honest to God. My boss gave him money at the Lake Geneva house. Put it a briefcase. For a fifty-million-dollar library annex."

"Bill did that. You're kidding."

Alice laughed. "He told me once when he was drunk at some party. I worked on that design commission."

"How much did he give him?" I asked.

"Twenty thousand," Alice added. "We made a million and a half fee on it."

"Bill was such a straight arrow with his five prep school kids, and that coiffured wife," I said. Now it was my turn to laugh.

"Was it cash? Hundred-dollar bills?"

Alice shrugged her shoulders, "I don't know, probably. What else would you put in a briefcase? Your wife's jewelry?"

I told her he could go to jail for that. It was a felony.

"I don't know. Bill was president of Colter Anderson for twenty-five years and we did tons of city and state buildings. I'll bet that wasn't the only time he paid somebody off for the business."

Fascinated at what she had said, I shook my head in disapproval. "Parties and vacations, that's one thing, but cold, hard cash, that's way different."

"I don't think he was the only one doing it. All the bigger architecture firms with that kind of money to throw around did it too. Most of Chicago is on the take. It's always been that way."

"But Billy-boy is such a good Catholic, so damn sanctimonious. He has a son at Notre Dame, for God's sake.

"Two," Alice mentioned, "the oldest and the one behind him. The oldest is in law school."

I snapped my fingers and turned to her: "Alice, you should write about that bribe and spin it into some strange web where this character like Bill commits murder, something like that to cover his tracks."

"Too close to home," she said, "I'm better off with characters I don't know."

"You're a good writer, follow your instincts."

She shook her head no and got up to refresh her drink from the scotch bottle in the alcove. I tried to prolong the subject, but she stood up, and said, "I'm tired, I'm going to bed. Maybe read a little."

Smiling I waved as she moved into the bedroom. I got out of the chair and stood in front of the window watching rain hit the pavement of the street below weaving its way down the hill toward the bay.

We are both terribly unhappy I thought as I looked down on the shiny blackness of the city street. And we don't know how to change that. It seems we're both afraid to say it aloud, so we keep it hidden.

For reasons unknown, Alice went back to the bribery tale of her old boss Bill, and she created a character that closely approximated Billy Burke. He was a working-class Irish kid from Chicago who was sent to Rice during World War II and left as an architect. As chance would have it, he later joined this blue stocking firm of architects founded in 1907. When the last Colter family member retired, he made forty-year-old Billy president over the heads of several other prominent firm architects. They all left in protest to the upstart.

99

Billy's salary quadrupled within a week. The first thing he did was move out of his Rodgers Park two-flat and bought a Georgian house in fashionable Winnetka alongside the lake. Three years after that, Billy bought a spacious ranch-style second home on Lake Geneva and joined the moneyed-class.

Ruled by his unwavering Catholic morality, Billy fathered six children with the North Shore debutant he had courted and married. They were avid churchgoers and sent their children to upscale Catholic academies, and later to Notre Dame, and its sister school, St. Mary's and to Boston College. They were model parents of their time. In fact, once a year the Chicago Roman Catholic Cardinal would grace their dinner table. Of course, Joan, his always coiffed wife was active in a half-dozen Chicago diocesan charities.

If Billy bent the rules, so be it, others did. That is the way Chicago operates, and it's best to learn those lessons early. The second mayor Daley was among their friends. And they had spent summer weekends at his Indiana Dunes house.

Billy became a sailor too and joined the Chicago yacht club. Within two years he put his sailboat into competition for the annual Mackinaw race. All these high jinks cost money.

With no hesitation, Billy Burke stripped the old-line firm of its ready cash and cut architects from the payroll. He built his own empire while at the same time, pretending it was the Thirties or Forties when they were the only game in town. And Billy paid bribes to city and state officials when he knew the people on the other end were on the take. He learned who those players were early on. It was this secret code among architects.

This impetus of Alice's past took over. She was writing day and night. She was determined to craft a novel about that corruption. Billy Burke became her poster boy. To the world, he was as clean as a hound's tooth when all the time his hands were dirtied.

She was less concerned with what he had done than why he did it. That was what she tried to fathom. She had been close to Billy, and he liked her, promoted her over others at the firm.

He was a devout Catholic who had pulled himself up by his bootstraps from the Southside Irish ghetto. He created a polished exterior perhaps to match his wife's pedigree. Maybe Billy was just an ambitious street kid who learned that one bent the rules a little to succeed. His public façade never changed. He could and would lie to the Cardinal's face without shame. The reason of it all might have started there. Alice was less interested in the nature of the crime itself than how Billy Burke might sin without remorse.

For two months, Alice wrote feverishly about him as her everyman character. She produced a biting and compelling novel of good and evil. I begged her to let me read it, but she refused, telling me again that was bad luck. She insisted that it was not the type of literature that would hold my interest.

The worst part was for the whole time, she was mostly drunk. She was not falling down drunk but slurring her words. It seemed that only whiskey could fuel her creativity.

She sent the novel to her old literary agent friend, who did read it. The woman said it was raw and beautiful, though commercial publishers wouldn't want it. Her only hope for print was someone like Grove, or maybe Milkweed press. They released about a dozen books each and wanted some celebrity along with the submission such as a fading movie career, or even prison. They required that brand of gravitas.

The book rejection propelled Alice further down the rabbit hole. I tried to talk her out of it to no avail. Slowly she retreated even further into herself.

"You've got to keep trying other publishers, and agents. Send out some letters. Make a few calls. Everybody gets turned down the first time."

"Bullshit," she said. "Laura told me the truth, nobody wants it."

"That's a sample of one person; give it two weeks of effort. Then call it quits."

Alice shook her head vigorously. "I can accept the fact that I can't write. I can be an architect again."

"Please give it a little more time, a week of letters and calls."

"I'm finished with it."

ABALONE

The subsequent weeks leading to Thanksgiving were morbid. I suggested we go Mendocino for the holiday. We could rent a cottage and hike some trails. In the end, we did nothing. We prepared a Thanksgiving turkey breast and some vegetables for the two of us. Later that afternoon we walked down to Aquatic Park

Sitting on the sea wall at the park, I asked Alice, "Are you happy here? It doesn't seem that way. Is our great migration a failure?"

She didn't answer immediately but pulled me up by the hand and told me she wanted to walk some more. She wanted to walk the trail through Fort Mason to the Golden Gate Bridge.

For the next fifteen minutes, we walked silently picking our way through hilly Fort Mason onto the sandy Crissy Field toward the bridge. Under the Golden Gate, Alice tried to skim flat stones on the water, and they kept sinking. "I can't even do that," she lamented.

I tried to smile, and said, "I have an idea. Let's get an Irish Coffee at the Buena Vista, it's not that far, and it might cheer everyone up." Unfortunately, it didn't work.

At the office I rented downtown I ran into the Embarcadero complex manager. She was a young woman in her late twenties that I had joined for lunch once or twice.

"I have a surprise for you," she said. "Wait here, I'll be right back."

When she returned, she was carrying a damp burlap bag. "It's the end of the day, so I figure you can carry this home," she said handing it to me. The bag was heavy, and it felt as if it was filled with rocks.

"What is it?" I asked, about to open it and look inside.

"My boyfriend works on the fishing boats and dives a lot too. He was up in Mendocino for the opening of abalone season. He brought a lot back with him. I'm lucky if I can eat one. You say you cook fish, well, here's your chance."

It was a long walk home, so I took a taxi with this load of shells weighing me down.

Alice was in her office, the spare bedroom. I called to her that I had a special treat for dinner. I would tell her when it was ready.

"That's fine," she answered without much enthusiasm.

Truth is, I had never cooked abalone, but I'd read about it. Because the shellfish is large and can get rubbery, you need to steam it first for a long time.

"Can you wait two hours?" I yelled out to her, and she said she could.

The first thing I did was throw the closed abalone shells into a steamer and let them sweat for an hour. By then the large shells were open, and I could remove the sea creature, which was six, or seven times the size of a large clam. With a sharp knife, I trimmed the liver, guts, mouth and skirt from the body. I sliced the meat thinly into narrow strips and put it aside.

Then, I made a salsa sauce. I ground together coriander, parsley, lemon zest and juice, capers and chili, and dribbled in some extra virgin olive oil.

I got a cast iron pan and put it on high heat. I added an ounce of butter and cooked it until it was brown. Then I threw in the abalone strips and cooked them for less than a minute. I added the sauce to the abalone and fried it for another thirty seconds and stirring until well mixed. At last I poured the concoction back into the shells. I put a basket of toasted bread on the table, and the meal was ready.

When Alice came to the table, she smiled and ate two pieces of the toast with the abalone. She said it was tasty, and that was all I could expect, I guess.

This then was the abrupt end of The Year of Cooking Fish. I admit it had been a colossal failure. There was little joy left at the table anymore. Sally might have helped, but she was far away and the two of us ate in silence.

******

San Francisco didn't work out. Alice was housebound and deeply depressed drinking more than ever. Now it seemed an uncontrollable addiction. We returned to Chicago in utter defeat. A place where she had family and friends, and where I thought there was some possibility of getting help to break the self-destructive cycle.

We moved into a lovely prewar apartment on Lake Shore Drive across the street from Belmont Harbor. We began to have friends over for dinner. It was a start, and I hoped that this familiarity of place and people would push her to curb the drinking. It didn't. By this time, she started in the morning when I left for the office and continued all day.

When I would return at night, she was already drunk. Sometimes she was asleep. Or did she pass out? I didn't know which most of the time.

Friends would say nothing to her about it. I was the only one left to complain, and that was obviously pointless. After two months, she had a minor accident with the car. And she had fallen several times on her way to the store a block away to purchase liquor.

I would learn later that whiskey bottles were hidden all over the apartment. If I had been monitoring one bottle, she had another nearby. By the day's end, she was often violently sick and vomited frequently. The only time Alice stopped drinking was when her parents visited. After they left, she would continue drinking into the night.

Then it happened. It was a Saturday, and I had lingered during the morning with a coffee on the couch looking out the window at the great lake, my thoughts racing. She came onto the couch next to me and put her head on my shoulder.

"If you don't help me, I'm going to kill myself," she said tearfully. "I can't stop drinking and there's only one way out. I hate looking at myself in the mirror, what I've become. I've turned into a vulgar drunk. Help me."

I couldn't hold my own tears back and held her closely. "Stay there," I said, "here's what we'll do," and I went into the pantry and brought back a phone book.

Quickly going to the Yellow Pages I found the Addiction heading. My eyes scanned the page until I found a small ad that read, Women's Recovery Program at Columbus Hospital. I quickly read what was offered, and pointed to it, looking at her.

"We'll do this, alright?" I asked, looking deeply into her tortured eyes.

"Yes," she answered, and I immediately dialed the number. A social worker answered. I told her about Alice, and our eagerness to seek help.

"That's the first step," the woman said in a kindly voice. She invited us to come by that next morning for an orientation. She told us it was an outpatient recovery program. The women who attended stayed there each weekday for six hours, and then were free to come home.

The woman said: "We have doctors, economists, lawyers, and housewives, all suffering and seeking to be healed."

At ten, the next morning we walked the three blocks to the hospital. Alice's world changed as she went through that revolving door.

This wasn't a happy ending. Alice's sobriety came after the six months, and on the outside, she appeared to be healthy. She played tennis at friend's club once a week, and there seemed to be projects where she had an interest.

******

Soon after a California friend called me and urged me to come back knowing we didn't want to leave San Francisco in the first place. It was me as I saw her drifting away fueled by excessive drinking. Maybe she would have killed herself as she later told me she might. Nothing made sense during that period. We went back.

We found a beautiful cedar-shingle hillside house in Sausalito, something out of a magazine. It had views of the bay and a back garden of rosemary. We bought a sailboat, having learned to sail on Lake Michigan, and kept it moored ten minutes away at the closest marina to town.

Weekend sails seemed to be the answer, and then they weren't. Before long, Alice lost interest, and rarely wanted to go out on the water. She told me that she needed more time to pull herself together, and then she could find a writing job. But she never left the house except for her Alcoholic Anonymous meetings, which she never missed. There were two every week, one for women only.

To have some small social life, I asked her to invite some friends from her AA group to our house. Several women and a couple men joined us for the occasional dinner. The conversations were always guarded, and sobriety stories became regular dinner conversation. I didn't really participate much in conversation though I listened and smiled in an attempt to be a friendly host.

We had extra bedrooms, so friends from Chicago were more likely to visit. We entertained about a half dozen friends. Even my mother came for a visit. She knew nothing about Alice's drinking, and I felt compelled to keep her in the dark.

The best visit of all was Sally's trip for a week. The two of us sailed a few afternoons. Out on the water, she was talkative, asking me, "What's wrong with Alice? I know about the drinking, but there's something else."

I attempted an explanation without much confidence, but all I could say was that it was common for changes when alcoholics finally got sober.

"Emotionally, I think it's a real roller coaster for Alice," I told Sally. "I try to stay out of the way."

"Not much fun for you," Sally added with a look of concern on her face.

"No, it isn't. Sometimes I'm so frustrated I want to scream. I'm always walking on eggshells. Honestly, I don't know what I can do or can't."

At that point, we dropped the subject. Sally told me Joyce had a cancer diagnosis, and it wasn't good.

"I'm glad I can spend this school year with her before I go to Dallas. It might be her last." Sally was a sweetheart. She had turned into a thoughtful young woman despite the craziness around her, especially that caustic mother. Joyce had softened that a bit.

When we got home from sailing, Alice had made a Mexican meal with beef tacos. Sally looked at me smiling, "What, no mystery fish?"

I smiled back and was the only one I think who appreciated the irony.

Alice asked about college and Sally told her she was going to study political science with plans possibly for law school afterward. The conversation was warm, but truthfully, it was as we were all strangers at the table, being careful to ask insightful questions of each other. Not surprisingly, nobody inquired about me at all, work, sailing or otherwise.

On the day before Sally's flight back, Alice proposed a hike in the Marin Headlands for just the two of them. They packed a picnic lunch for the trip. It was their time together.

After Sally left, the days continued as before. Alice told me she needed more time before she was healthy enough to look for work. I told her to take as long as she needed.

One day I came home early on the ferry from San Francisco, as nothing at the office required my attention. Alice returned two hours later, looking flush as she came into the door.

"I need to talk to you," she insisted, this pinched look on her face. "Sit down."

Sitting down on a chair with my hands folded on my lap, I waited for what she wanted to say. She was nervously pacing in front of the big windows overlooking Richardson Bay Harbor.

The silence seemed to last forever, and finally I said, "Well?"

"I want a divorce," she barked out. "There I've said it. That's what I want."

A look of shock on my face, I leaned forward, and chose my words carefully, "Is there someone else?"

"Yes, and I love him," she uttered almost out of breath.

"It's that guy you talk about all the time from AA, the screenwriter."

"It doesn't matter. You have no passion for me anyway. You'll be better off."

Now I could only look at her in anger and shook my head. "How long has this been going on?"

She tossed her head back and said, "For a while."

I knew he had a studio apartment two streets above the house. Now the anger came out, and I laughed. "That explains the red face when you came in. You just got out of bed."

"You can move out, or I will, it really doesn't matter to me." She wanted to be angry though she couldn't.

"I'll move down to the boat," I told her. At that moment, it struck me hard that whatever we once had, those plans and promises had vanished. I inherited nothing in their place. It had all happened in two minutes; that was the end. Painful as it was, I moved onto the sailboat, and weeks turned into months with nothing said between us. We didn't even talk about Sally who was now in college and doing well.

That shiny Catalina sailboat resembled a well-planned city apartment. Albeit it was small but with a kitchen and bathroom, salon area with a table and benches. I slept in the berth in the bow. It was a five-minute walk to cafes on the town square and to regular ferry service to San Francisco. My commute to and from the office each day remained unchanged.

I had left a comfortable craftsman-type house where we had a spacious living room with a fireplace and bay views plus a small Asian tiered garden of rosemary bushes behind. And I had created a tiny art studio in the basement where on most nights while Alice watched television in her office/bedroom, I painted abstract canvases. Now living on the narrow sailboat, I sorely missed the studio. It had taken me away from the madness and distance we experienced with each other. It became a refuge.

What Alice did with her newfound companion, I didn't know. At the end of the sixth month of our separation, she emptied the house into a storage locker and moved into a small apartment a half block away. She found it through another AA friend who had left the Bay Area and was going back to his native New Zealand.

She told me that any reconciliation was only in my imagination over coffee at a dockside café, on one of the few days we had seen each other.

"This is over," she announced, "I see no point for us to talk again, honestly. I'm filing for divorce."

There was little of her earlier softness toward me, that morning together was as cold as any corporate business deal, I had done in my career. It was short and to the point, and with no wasted time.

"I don't want to go to court," she added. "We can mediate here in Marin, the two of us and our lawyers. Sit down and talk it through."

"That's it, then," I said as emotionlessly as I felt at the time.

Looking at her, I remained silent for perhaps another thirty seconds and finished the coffee that remained in the cup in front of me.

"Really, there's no need for us to meet anymore. I don't think it's healthy. This forever friends thing is something you see in movies. It just prolongs the hurt."

"There's Sally too," I introduced into the conversation.

"I'll always love her, and she'll be a part of my life. If you allow it."

"Nobody suffers from too much love," I said. "I'll never be in the way."

She smiled, but something about it was pained. It was hardly genuine. "You're a good man. It didn't work. I'm sorry." After that comment she rose from the small table, "I must go. Goodbye," and she walked to the parking lot and her car.

I didn't say goodbye to her but simply nodded my head in acknowledgement. After she left, I got another coffee and sat there for about a half an hour lost in my thoughts. I replayed the tape of our entire life together.

"What did I do wrong?" I asked myself in a whisper. I couldn't quite identify whatever it was that had made this breakup occur.

I could blame it on the alcohol and the addiction she suffered, but was that enough of a reason? I convinced myself it was, some of it, at least. I considered myself guilty too, and the awful distance I'd created between us, unconsciously, or otherwise.

Getting ready to leave the cafe, I hadn't noticed, though now I saw she'd put a five-dollar bill under her coffee mug to pay for her share of the bill. That was typical of how her mind worked. She was responsible to a fault and then she wasn't.

I drove my old '74 Alfa convertible back to the boat, the cool Northern California morning air caressing my face. I figured a part of me was broken, off balance, but I knew it had been broken long before.

So without much thought, I put all those creatures of the sea out of my mind. I can't tell you when I next ate fish.

Bruce Colbert is an actor, filmmaker, and author of books of fiction and poetry, most recently *The Hutchisons*. A former wartime Navy Seabee and ocean sailor, he lives in coastal Alabama. For more information, see http://www.brucecolbert.info/